*Guardians of Zion: Foundations of Faith*
Copyright © 2017 by Michael Chrobak

Seneschal Publishing; Oakley, California
www.seneschalpublishing.com
Twitter: @SeneschalBooks

Book Cover Artist:
Kristyn / Drop Dead Designs
http://www.dropdeaddesigns.com

ISBN paperback: 978-0-9981350-8-3
ISBN eBook: 978-0-9981350-9-0

Second Paperback Edition

Printed in the United States of America

For my children
Thank you for calling me 'Dad'

# INTRO

What is faith? The Bible tells us faith is "*…the assurance of things hoped for, the conviction of things not seen.*" (Hebrews 11:1). But what does that really mean? In short, it means we know something is going to happen even before it happens. Not like the ability to predict the future, but close. For example, we have faith that the sun will rise tomorrow, but we aren't certain of this fact. Anything can happen between sunset and sunrise. Perhaps the sun does not rise tomorrow, at least for us. In truth, only God knows for sure. We only have hope and faith.

St. Augustine once said:

*"To one who has faith, no explanation is necessary.*
*To one without faith, no explanation is possible."*

This is the dichotomy. When you have faith, the *how* doesn't matter, only the *why*. But without faith, neither matter. In between these poles is where most people find themselves. Like the Disciple Thomas in the Bible, we all have doubts. We are torn between needing to know and having faith to rest in the unknowing. This is the difference between being free and feeling trapped, between living and dying, between love and fear.

This is the world of the main character, Brother Thomas. He is torn between the freedom to be who he is meant to be and the slavery of following the ways of the world. It's not that he doesn't have faith, it's that he isn't aware that he does. He has difficulty making the leap. He wants to trust that everything happens for a reason and that he has purpose. But the events of his life are chaotic. He can't see the blessings that are buried deep in the pain and frustration he feels. And so he goes on a quest to find the answers. He thinks he will find the answers down the most convenient road, but real treasure is never buried where it can be easily found. His journey will take him through some of the most difficult and trying moments of life, times when he will question why he was even born.

It's the same for us. We go through life wondering, *"Why did this happen to me?"* We pray for release from struggle and yet, if not for struggle, we would never become who we are meant to be. To grow, we must walk the balance between knowledge and surrender. We must learn to accept everything that comes, not from a point of resignation or defeat, but with the realization there is something God wants us to learn. At first, we must learn to learn, from every moment we experience; each encounter, every blessing, and every pain. It's all there to lead, guide, and help us become who we were created to be.

Why must we walk this path? Well, there are two alternates, neither of which seem palatable to me. The first is a life where nothing matters, where nothing we do makes any sense or is of any use. And the other is a world so rigid that we don't have a choice. We know who we are meant to be from the day we are born, and we simply go about doing what we were meant to do. Like a robot. No, the only life that, to me, seems to be the one worth living is the one we already have. Do we have a purpose? By all means. Do we know what that purpose is? Not at first, but we will. Besides, an adventure is about the travel between point A and point B, not the destination. Most of the experiences of life are found in the transition between where we are and where we are meant to be. At every point along the road, we have the choice to move towards the life God is calling us to or to continue living the life this world says we should.

This is the reason I chose Faith as the Fruit of the Holy Spirit this first book is based on. Without faith, nothing else really matters. I'm inviting you to take this walk with Brother Thomas. Set aside any doubts you have about your own faith, and just trust the process. I honestly believe, regardless of who you are, that you will find the answers you seek within these pages. This is why I am writing these books from the perspective of fantasy. True knowledge cannot be taught through the mind. It must be felt within the heart. That is where the essence of faith will blossom to the greatest potential.

And that is my hope. That is my faith. That these books will help you better understand what life is really about. That they will help you find your purpose, or at least set your feet on the right path. I would love to hear your stories. At the back of this book, you will find my contact information. Feel free to write, or email, or text, or whatever new methods of communication we might have around at the point these books finally find themselves in your hands. I wish you the best – now and always. Now, let's pack our bags and get ready for an adventure!

# PART ONE

*We always find that those who walked closest to Christ were those who had to bear the greatest trials.*

*— St. Teresa of Avila*

# CHAPTER ONE
## FROM THE DARKNESS

Thomas sat motionlessly, his eyes fixed on the back of the chair in front of him. Around him, the room faded into shadows, as if the darkness he had hidden from most of his life had finally caught up. It surrounded him from all sides, cutting him off from everything he believed was real. Nothing mattered anymore but the thoughts racing through his mind, and the back of that chair. He knew the room where he sat still existed, but that didn't matter. He knew it was still filled with dozens of teens his age, but they no longer mattered. He knew the murmur of sounds whispering past his ears was coming from Father Dominic, but the words carried by those sounds passed without meaning. For now, all he had was the spot on the chair in front of where he sat, and the darkness closing in. As long as his eyes remained fixed on that chair, he could hold off the darkness. At least, he hoped he could. He didn't want to disappear like the rest of the room.

At first, Thomas had listened to Father Dominic's talk with mock interest. This was already the fourth talk he had heard this weekend, and it was only Saturday morning. The first one was on Friday night, shortly after they had arrived at the retreat center. The teens were all anxious, restless. It had taken some time to settle everyone down. Eventually, Amanda, the Youth Minister at his church, got things under control, and the retreat began. That first talk had started with a boring video, followed by what Thomas felt was a more-than-depressing song.

Finally, one of the young adults had shared their story. She talked about how she had gotten involved in drugs in junior high, and how she had turned from being a straight 'A' student to barely making it to class by high school. The product, she had said, of having the wrong group of friends, and a weak moral compass. She shared how she had been arrested for shoplifting, twice, and how she had stolen some of her mom's jewelry, all for just 'one more high'. She shared how she had finally found God, not in the back of a church with hands held in prayer, but in the back of a police car with hands held in cuffs. She had been fifteen at the time.

The next two talks followed the same format. They started with a short video, followed by a song most likely chosen for its strong potential to make people cry. He never did, though; cry, that is. He wouldn't freely give away his emotions to these people. He didn't know them, and he definitely didn't believe they cared about him. They were just doing their job. They were nice enough people, they just didn't rate admission to the hidden secrets of his soul. At least, not while Thomas was still unsure what he would find there himself, should he ever choose to take a look.

For those first three talks, Thomas did his best to appear interested, but to him, it was just the same stuff they did every Sunday night after church. It certainly didn't make him feel any more like he wanted to be a Catholic. And it definitely didn't answer his questions about God. And so, he would listen, but only halfway. He really didn't care. He just wanted to get through the weekend and get back home. After this, there were no more sacraments his parents could force him to get, and no more Religious Education classes he would have to take.

In the Catholic tradition, there are four sacraments an individual receives to complete their initiation in the faith. The first three, Baptism, First Reconciliation and Holy Communion, were all completed while he was still considered to be too young to choose for himself. And so his parents had chosen. But this final one, the Sacrament of Confirmation, was supposed to be his choice. Even so, his parents had made it very clear exactly which choice he was going to make. But it was almost over. He just had to get through this retreat, pick a service project, and wait for the Bishop to proclaim him confirmed. In another month or two, he would be done with church.

But somehow this fourth talk was different. A few minutes into Father Dominic's talk, his interest began to pique. The talk itself was about God's Grace, which was something Thomas really didn't understand. Yet, Father Dominic spoke in a way that made the clouds of his confusion drift apart. There were a lot of things about church that Thomas didn't get. For one, he didn't think that God, if there was a God, would let good people suffer. It just didn't make sense. Yet, as Father Dominic talked about his own life and the struggles of becoming a priest, Thomas began to see a connection. When Father Dominic shared how God sometimes gives trials in life not to make people suffer, but to strengthen them for future challenges, Thomas had started to think. He hadn't faced many trials in his life. His parents hadn't been divorced, like a good number of the kids in this room. He hadn't used drugs or alcohol yet, like a good number of kids in this room. His parents were hard working people and were dedicated volunteers at church. He had grown up in a pretty affluent neighborhood with just about everything he could want, and more than he needed.

Which was what had started him thinking. As he recalled all the people on the retreat who had shared struggles from their lives so far, he began to wonder why he had been so blessed. It wasn't like he was some awesome Catholic or anything. He only went to church when his parents made him, or when it was required as part of the Confirmation program. He never read the Bible unless he had to look something up during one of his classes. He definitely didn't know how to pray. And, to be honest, he didn't even think about God all that much. So why had he been so blessed? Why had he never experienced the kind of pain and suffering faced by a lot of the people on this retreat? He had heard stories this weekend that made him wonder how some of the teens here had got through their trials. Like Jonathan, who had talked about the loss of his parents and his older sister in a car crash when he was only twelve. Or Terry, who had shared about his dad who was put in jail when Terry was just seven. He had also talked about his mom who, Terry admitted, was always drunk.

Thomas began to question why God had given him such an easy life when he hadn't given anything back to God. The more he thought about how blessed he was, the more he had felt that darkness grow. He had felt unworthy of everything he had in life, began to feel guilty for never once thanking God for any of it. He realized he had never thanked his parents most of the time, either. It became clear how spoiled he had been, and how much he really didn't deserve the life he had. He began to think that, in some ways, he was probably the biggest sinner on the retreat. Here were all these people living with the struggles of their lives, and yet they were praising God. And here he was, without hardly a care, not giving a damn about his faith. The deeper these feelings of un-worthiness dug into his heart, the darker the room had become. It had spread from the outside in, growing darker and more ominous with each new thought. Thomas feared it would swallow him whole.

Now, he felt light-headed, nauseous, and his breaths were shallow and quick. All he wanted was to get out of the room, fast. Sensing movement around him, he realized Father Dominic's talk had ended. Amanda had just released the teens for a break. That was the chance he needed. Thomas stood up, feeling dizzy and weak. He headed for the door. It felt impossible to breathe while he was inside this room. The weight of the air was crushing him. He pushed past the crowd of teens at the snack table. He could feel the darkness around him gathering, racing him to the door. He had to get there first. His feet crossed the threshold, stumbling over something he hadn't seen. As he fell forward, fingers of darkness grabbed at his shirt. But he was out. He desperately gasped for air, ignoring the laughter around him from those who had seen him fall. A few had even flung a few insults his way regarding his graceful exit. Thomas didn't respond. He simply got up and walked as slowly as he could manage towards the corner of the building. All he wanted was to get away; from the darkness, the crowd, the laughter, and the noise. It was too much for him to handle.

As he walked, he felt the darkness behind him, following him. He swore he heard it whisper, "Run!" Not wanting to look back, afraid of what he might find if he did, his feet began moving faster.

Suddenly, one of the adults called out, "Thomas! Don't go too far! This is just a five-minute break. Come right back, okay?"

He waved over his shoulder, hoping that would be enough to prevent them from following. The last thing he wanted was to be followed. Just to be sure, he yelled back, "I'm just going to the cabin for a sec. I forgot my, uh, notebook."

He dared not turn back, not even for a moment. He didn't know what he feared more, the bitter cold of the darkness he had felt in the room, or being followed by one of the adults. Why he worried about being followed, he couldn't understand. He was just taking a quick walk to calm his nerves, right? In ten more steps, he would be at the corner of the building, then he would stop, catch his breath, and calm down. It was probably just some kind of panic attack. His mom got them all the time. He was just having one of those, right?

Five more steps.

Two.

One.

He reached the corner, but instead of stopping, Thomas kept on. Behind him, he could sense the darkness, pushing him further along. Onward he went, passing the end of one building, then the next. The light gray paint on this building was peeling away, revealing a variety of colors beneath. That's how he felt right now. Like he was peeling away. The walls he hid behind were fading fast, leaving gaping holes where anyone could see his soul. He couldn't stop here, not by these buildings. Maybe farther down. His feet skimmed across the top of the dirt path, barely touching down as he raced faster and faster.

Buildings flew past now, one after the next. He pressed on, past the bathrooms and the dining hall. Surely he was going to stop soon. Maybe when he got to the basketball courts he could sit down and relax. Yet each time he reached a point where he thought he would stop, his feet just kept going, continuing to gain speed. Even faster now, the darkness lurking behind. Again, he heard the voice. This time, it was more than just a whisper.

*"Run, Thomas! That's right. Run! Keep running. To the end of the trail. Out into the field. Just keep going. Don't look back, don't stop. Just run!"* the darkness demanded.

Thomas was having trouble breathing again, and his feet began to stumble. They were moving too fast to leave prints in the dusty path, and yet, a moment later, his pace quickened even more. He passed one more building, then the trail turned to his right. It flowed down a small hill into a clearing. In the middle of the clearing stood one last building.

The chapel.

He had been down this way earlier in the morning for prayer. He knew that, beyond the chapel, the trail ended at a small gate. On the other side was a road leading out from the denser woods surrounding the retreat center. He knew from the safety briefing they had received Friday night that it would be miles until he would find another building down that road. Out there, somewhere, he would find the abandoned mines of the old mining camp. The buildings he had just passed originally made up the small town that housed the families of the miners. Other than the rolling hills, pockets of trees, and whatever animals he might find, nothing else was out this way.

As the distance between him and the end of the trail quickly disappeared, he noticed the gate was open. It had been shut and locked earlier, that he was sure. One of the other teens had been caught playing with the lock. Thomas wondered who had opened it and if they were still around. The last thing he wanted was for some adult to see him and ask what was wrong. As he neared the chapel, he noticed the front door stood open as well. Afraid now that someone must be near, and wanting nothing less than to be seen, his panic turned to tears. The trail he was on would pass right by the chapel's open door. What would he do if someone was inside? What would he do if they called out to him? In his desperation, he prayed he would find the chapel empty as he passed.

Wait…he prayed?

*He prayed!*

His mind grabbed hold of that thought. He had just prayed! It was short, quick, to the point, but it was a prayer. Six simple words. *"God, don't let anyone see me."* It may have been the first time since his First Communion classes that his voice had been used to pray. The darkness that had been following him suddenly felt less foreboding. He sensed this might be his way out. As his feet hit the dirt path just outside the door to the chapel, he prayed aloud, almost shouting, "God, please help me!"

The words barely off his tongue, two things happened at once. The first was a strong gust of wind plunging in from his left. It struck him so hard, he almost fell. His body bent to the right as the wind spun him about. He tried to catch his footing but stumbled instead - right through the open front door. At the same time, he felt the darkness disappear. One moment it was there, and then the next, it was gone. He began to gasp for air. A sharp pain in his side told him he must have struck the door on the way through, causing the automatic hinge to close. The door slammed shut hard. His hands grabbed unsuccessfully at the corners of the wooden pews. Thomas' legs felt like Jell-O, his knees buckling with each step, and then they simply gave up trying. He hit the floor, hard, landing on his stomach, arms stretched out wide, face on the ground. Thomas slid across the wooden floor until he came to rest, perfectly centered in the one small patch of sunlight that poured in through the cross-shaped, stained glass window behind the altar.

And then, his mind went black.

# Chapter Two
## CONVERSION

Thomas gasped, the air returning to his lungs in great, gulping breaths. His legs were quivering. He felt tired; no, he felt exhausted. And he felt pain. It screamed at him from his left shoulder. His forehead throbbed, too. He gently rubbed the spot where his head had struck the wooden floor. There was definitely a lump. But luckily, no blood. As bad as it felt, at least it didn't need immediate attention. As he continued assessing his injuries, he became aware of something else. He was no longer afraid. Somehow he felt safer than he had ever felt before. Slowly, he opened his eyes. It took some time for his brain to register where he was, and then the memory of his uncontrollable run came rushing back, causing his head to throb even more.

He didn't know if the darkness was still there, lurking outside the chapel, waiting for him, but he really didn't care. He would lie where he was on the floor all day if he had to. Lie there until someone finally noticed he hadn't come back. Amanda would call off the list of names like usual. They would figure out he was gone. She'd most likely send one of the adults to look for him. It might take time, but eventually, they would find him. He wondered how much trouble he would be in, and if he would be able to talk his way out of it. But that would come later. Until then, he would just lay here on the floor, with the late afternoon sun cascading through the stain glass window, shooting rainbows across the room.

After a few long moments passed, the glow of the sun changed from the warm, stained glass hues to brilliant white. Thomas sensed a presence around him as if the light was holding him somehow. As the warmth of the golden white light penetrated deep within him, he felt better. His breathing returned to normal, the pain in his shoulder and head weren't as strong, and his legs had stopped quivering. He lay there feeling his strength returning, with no trace of the panic he had felt. Thomas took one more deep breath in, holding it as long as he could, and then let it slide soundlessly past parched lips.

Water.

He could really, really use a bottle of water right now. And maybe a snack or two. He was starving! Some chips, a couple cookies, maybe a handful of red vines. Heck, he'd even settle for some of the healthy crap Amanda had put out. Apples, or those little boxes of raisins, maybe some trail mix. There would be plenty of snacks on the table back in the large group room, right next to a smaller table holding rows of plastic cups, one with his name on it. Next to that, he knew there would be one of those dispensers with a big blue jug of water perched on top. Thomas had watched them replace that bottle twice since Friday night. He began to wonder how much water a hundred teens would drink over the course of three days.

And then something happened that had never happened to him before. A scripture verse passed through his mind.

*Everyone who drinks of this water will be thirsty again,*
*but whoever drinks of the water that I will give him*
*will never be thirsty again.*

He must have heard someone use that verse during one of the talks earlier. Or perhaps it had been part of the readings from Morning Prayer. That's the thing about only paying attention half-way. Things had a way of getting stuck in your head, and you never knew where they came from. He said the verse aloud, pondering the concept of never being thirsty again, then admitted out loud, "I could use some of that water right about now."

A voice replied, "I was hoping you would ask."

Thomas raised his head, turning in the direction of the voice. No one was there.

"Hello?" he called out.

"Do not fear, Thomas," the voice responded, seeming to come from everywhere at once. "You're safe in here. The darkness you felt is gone. This is my house. It won't touch you here. Rest easy now."

Thomas nervously looked around, his eyes opening as wide as they could. "God? For real...is that you?" His voice shook uneasily.

The voice chuckled. "Oh, heavens no. I wouldn't dream of being that blessed."

Thomas heard a small scraping sound, like fabric dragging across the floor. He turned towards the door and saw Father Dominic entering the chapel. His long, brown robe dragging on the wooden floor as he walked.

"How...how'd you know about the darkness?" Thomas asked meekly.

"I was watching you during my talk. He really took you for a ride, didn't he?" Father Dominic replied.

"I'm sorry, I don't understand. How did you know it was a darkness? Who took me for a ride? And how'd you know I would be here?" Thomas pleaded, his mind filled with questions.

Father Dominic sat down on the floor near Thomas' feet before responding. He looked him over for a moment and then said, "Let's take those questions one at a time. As for how I knew you would be here? Well, I didn't. I just followed what seemed the most likely path. I checked just about every door on my way down. As for who it was that I think got you so upset? That's easy. He's been called the evil one, or the trickster. Simply put, it was the devil, the Angel of Darkness, Lucifer, Satan…whatever you want to call him.

"And as for how I knew it felt like darkness? Well, I could see that in the expression on your face. You see, I believe I've felt the same way once, years ago. He challenged you during my talk. Made you start to doubt yourself, to think you're not worthy, right? Consider yourself lucky. He doesn't pay much attention to those of little faith. No need to. They do a good job of doing his work for him on their own, although they don't know it."

Thomas wasn't sure he had heard him right.

"Are you telling me the devil is real? That he isn't just some fairytale or something? But really real?" Thomas shuddered.

"Oh, not in the flesh and blood like you or I. No, no, no, no. You'll never see him like I am seeing you right now. But that doesn't make him any less real than we are. More so, in fact, since he's been around so long. Oh, yes, he exists. He has become quite skillful in his deceptions over the generations, too. His greatest trick now is convincing people that he's not really there. A few generations ago, people prayed far more often for protection from him. Now we push away his deeds, label them something else. Mid-life crisis. Nervous breakdown. Antisocial disorder. We've become pretty good at taking the blame for why our lives seem out of control. All that New Age philosophy mumbo jumbo," Father Dominic shook his head slowly. "But he's there. Behind the scenes. Like the man behind the curtain in The Wizard of Oz. And just like that movie, he's not as powerful as he would like to be, not once he's been exposed, once the curtain has dropped.

"By the way," Father Dominic continued after a short pause, "You wouldn't mind sitting up, would you? You look awful uncomfortable."

Thomas realized he was still in the position he had been since he fell to the floor. Slowly, he pulled his left arm down to his chest, rolling over onto his side, and then sat up. He slid along the floor until his back was resting against one of the pews, and then he stretched out his arms and legs, taking in a deep breath and trying to stifle a yawn.

Father Dominic winced when he saw Thomas' face. "That's quite the bruise there. You sure you're okay?"

Thomas nodded. "It doesn't hurt much at all." He paused, reaching up to touch the spot where his head had struck the ground again. He was surprised to find that both the pain and the lump were gone. He had either never fallen, or had been here for longer than he thought.

"How long have I been down here, anyway?"

Father Dominic squinted as he looked at his watch. "Let's see, my talk ended around ten…so I guess a little over an hour now? It should be lunch soon."

So that's why he felt so hungry. He hadn't eaten since breakfast, which was at least four hours ago. Glancing back to Father Dominic, he asked, "You say the Devil doesn't bother people of little faith, huh?"

Father Dominic nodded his head. "That's right. He's more like a first responder in an emergency but in the opposite way. Where a paramedic will quickly judge the injuries and respond to the most injured first, the Devil judges by your faith, attacking hardest those he thinks are strongest. The weakest ones he just leaves alone. If he can knock out just a few of the faithful people, he can do quite a lot of damage to the church as a whole."

Thomas thought for a moment, then said, "Well, I don't know what he would want with me then. I would think my faith is one of the weakest on this retreat."

Father Dominic had a distant look in his eyes as if lost in thought, the slightest of smiles on his face.

"Don't underestimate what God has in store, Thomas," he offered. "You may well yet find a faith deeper than you could imagine."

Outside the chapel, the lunch bell rang crisp and clear, causing both men to turn towards the sound. Father Dominic stood up, reaching down to assist Thomas.

"Come," he said. "Let's talk more as we walk. I have a feeling you might be more in need of sustenance for your stomach than your soul right now."

Helping Thomas to his feet, Father Dominic turned and walked to the door. He held it open for Thomas to pass through.

Thomas stood momentarily in place, a part of him fearful that the panic would return once he left the building, and still another part afraid of what more Father Dominic might tell him. He was still skeptical of his worthiness to ever become someone of great faith or even someone of little faith. If he was completely honest with himself, until his experience today, there had never been reason to have faith at all. He wasn't sold yet on Father

Dominic's certainty that what happened had been some spiritual attack by an invisible, evil entity. That was just another way the church tried to keep believers from doing bad stuff, right? For now, he would simply call it what he thought it was all along. A panic attack, that's all.

He walked the few short steps to the door of the chapel, lingering once more at the threshold, his eyes locked on a small copper bowl half filled with water that was attached to the doors' frame. Sensing that Father Dominic was watching him, he came to the conclusion that, even if he really didn't believe…at least not yet…it couldn't hurt. Choosing to be safe rather than sorry, he quickly blessed himself with the water and stepped outside.

After a few steps, a question came to his mind. Without looking in the direction of Father Dominic, he asked, "Why did you choose to be a priest, Father? I know you may have shared during your talk, but, well, I really wasn't paying attention."

Father Dominic spoke gently, playing with the words. "Oh, I think when you look back at this morning, you'll find you captured a lot more than you think you did. But, to aid your memory now, I'll share it again."

He took a deep breath and then began.

"First, as I did in my talk, let me explain a bit more about the vocation of priesthood. I have a feeling you may need to understand this information as you mature. The term priesthood is a conjunction of two words: priest, which comes from the Greek word presbyteros, generally meaning an elder; and the suffix hood, which basically means a condition, or way of being. So, literally speaking, the term can be transcribed as someone who is in the condition of being an elder. Not in the sense of being old, but in the sense of being wise. Now, in the early days of the church, there was still great reverence held for those who had reached 'the age of wisdom,' much more respect than is given today, unfortunately. Over time, the term was applied to anyone considered mature enough to be put in charge, or left in a position responsible for the care of the members of the church."

Father Dominic glanced at Thomas to make sure he was listening, and then continued, "Today, we refer to priests as those who have the rights of Holy Orders and have taken sacred vows to live their life according to the precepts established by the Apostles, who were the original leaders of our church. There are different levels of Holy Orders. The First Order refers to Priests, Deacons or Brothers. The Second belongs to the Sisters, or Nuns, as they are sometimes called. Finally, there is the Third Order, which is for any member of the general public, known as lay persons; people like you who want to dedicate their life to Jesus' mission, but are unwilling or unable to take the vows of the First or Second Order. Now, the most recognized of those in the First Order are known as Diocesan priests. They typically are the ones you see wearing the black shirt with the little white square patch at the throat. Diocesan priests make promises of obedience and chastity, and they comprise the majority of the structure or hierarchy of the church. But some priests, such as myself, believe those promises are not enough and choose to live within a specific religious community. These religious communities are generally formed by the church to promote a certain lifestyle, modeled after the life of the individual whose name they bear. For example, I am a member of the Franciscan order and we choose to follow the example of Saint Francis."

He shook the fabric of his habit, holding the ends of his rope belt in one hand.

"The Franciscans, besides taking vows of chastity and obedience to the church, as do the Diocesan priests, also take a vow of poverty. Some of the other religious communities that also do this include the Claretians, who follow the life of St. Anthony Claret, then there are the Carmelites, or more specific, the Order of the Brothers of the Blessed Virgin Mary of Mount Carmel. And then you have the Dominicans, the Jesuits, the Salesians... the list goes on and on really. The important thing to remember is, not all priests take the vow of poverty. But we're getting off track just a bit. We'll talk more about this part at a later time I'm sure."

Father Dominic paused a moment.

"Now...as to why *I* became a priest...which was your original question ...well, I guess there came a point in my life where I just couldn't see any other way of living. Like you, I had deep questions about my faith, especially during my youth. I suppose most teens do. However, unlike most teens, I didn't just gloss over those questions, or push them to the back of my mind. I had to find answers, more like I was driven to find them, I guess. I simply had to know if the story of Jesus was real or not. I mean, it all sounded so mystical, so mysterious in ways. Could someone truly raise someone else from the dead, as Jesus did with Lazarus? Or could he really take a small amount of fish and bread and feed five thousand people? I guess I figured that, if he could do it, then maybe I could do it as well."

Father Dominic chuckled softly and then sighed deeply at the recollection of this memory. He glanced again at Thomas, giving him a broad smile.

"Ah...the aspirations of youth! So strange to think, after over twenty years in this ministry, that I was drawn to my vocation by the desire to perform some sort of magic trick with fish and bread! And you think you have little faith!"

Father Dominic shook his head.

Thomas said nothing out loud, but inside he was surprised by the openness and honesty of this man walking beside him. To think that a priest would have doubts about his faith! Thomas then recalled a memory of his own from his early childhood. Back then he had thought priests must come from a different place than 'normal' people did. Since he usually saw them only at church, he thought they didn't come from a family. To think of a priest having a mom or dad just seemed weird at the time.

He recalled how much simpler life was as a child, thinking of times when he had sat in church truly wanting to believe, honestly desiring to see Jesus face-to-face. At times, Thomas would pray that Jesus would show him a sign to let him know he was listening. He would pick out one of the votive candles in the rack on the side of the altar, silently asking Jesus to light it. Then he would patiently wait, his eyes locked on that candle, fully expecting it would ignite.

Other times he would pretend he had to use the bathroom, and instead would take the stairs to the basement where the church parties were held, asking Jesus to meet him there. He knew there wouldn't be anyone else in the basement while Mass was going on, so no one would see him talking to Jesus. But Jesus never showed, and those candles never lit. Perhaps that was when the doubts about his faith started. If only once he had seen even a brief moment of proof!

And now, to hear that Father Dominic also had questions about the legitimacy of his own faith, and yet still chose to dedicate his life to the priesthood, gave Thomas hope in the possibility of having his questions answered someday. As he reflected on these things, Father Dominic remained silent. Glancing up again, Thomas saw they were almost to the dining hall. By now, most of the teens had already made their way inside. The noise from the crowd of kids all talking at once amid the clatter of plastic trays, plates, bowls, and silverware increased in volume with every step. He didn't want his conversation with Father Dominic to end, but also didn't want anyone else to overhear. Perhaps sensing his desire, Father Dominic offered a solution.

"Why don't we continue this talk inside at one of the smaller tables? Unless you would prefer to eat with your friends?" he inquired.

Thomas replied hesitantly, not wanting to appear too interested.

"Yeah, sure. I guess I have a few more questions. We can grab a table back there."

He pointed to the back of the room where none of the teens he knew were seated nearby.

As they entered the dining hall, they headed in two different directions, with Father Dominic heading to where Amanda and the retreat leadership team sat. They all turned at once to where Thomas stood in line, most likely curious where he had disappeared, and yet obviously glad he had been found safe. He wondered if Father Dominic was telling them where he had found him, or if he shared anything about the conversation they had discussed so far. He felt a brief flash of nervous anxiety wash over him as these thoughts passed. Movement near him brought his attention back, as the line of teens waiting to be served began to move again, and Thomas turned back to the task of getting his meal. Though he couldn't rid himself of the feeling that he was being watched.

After gathering his selections, which included three hot dogs, two huge brownies and three cartons of milk, he caught sight of Father Dominic with a small plate of salad and fruit, sitting at a table up against the wall in the back of the room. Behind him, the bank of windows looked out over a swollen creek below. He took the chair across from the priest, attacking his meal ravenously. For a full minute or more Thomas sat there shoving food into his mouth, his eyes focused on the plate in front of him. Still feeling that he was being watched, he was reluctant to make eye contact with Father Dominic. Eventually, Thomas glanced up, only to find the priest sitting with his arms folded, his food untouched.

"Perhaps we should say grace first?" Father Dominic asked, smiling broadly.

Thomas could feel the blood rushing to his face. His jaw stopped mid-chew as he felt like crawling under the table. Swallowing the barely chewed mouthful, he put the carton of milk and the half-eaten hot dog back down, and then folded his hands and bowed his head.

"Why don't you lead us?" Father Dominic asked.

Thomas shot a look of fear back at him. Did he hear him right? Seriously? He wanted Thomas to pray? Wasn't that Father Dominic's job?

"I don't know what I would say," he admitted, hoping he could wiggle out of the request.

Father Dominic shrugged. "Words don't matter. God sees what's in your heart. Try just saying whatever comes to mind, say what you feel."

"I don't know, Father. I mean, I really don't pray that much – like ever, I guess," Thomas replied, still hoping to be let off the hook, but Father Dominic simply sat there, hands folded, head bowed, waiting for Thomas to start. With a deep sigh, Thomas licked his lips, wanting to be anywhere but at this table. Though, at least he wasn't up in front of the whole room like they had asked a few of the teens to do last night. That had been awkward, at best. Sensing there was no way out of this except to do what was expected of him, he cleared his throat.

"Uh…God?" he started. "Um…thanks for the food we have. And for the people who cooked it. And for the retreat people. And for the teens here too." Thomas said with lengthy pauses between.

He glanced at Father Dominic, seeing his head still bowed. Thomas thought perhaps there was more he was supposed to say, and so he went on.

"Oh…and thank you for Father Dominic. He's a pretty good guy. And…well…I guess I'm curious…like about what happened today and all. Like if that was you that pushed me into the chapel. And…well…if it was…I guess I should say thanks."

Feeling his throat start to tighten and his eyes begin to water, Thomas hastily added a quick 'amen' and went back to his meal. Shoving half of what was left of his hot dog into his mouth, he turned his head, pretending to look out the window. In reality, he just didn't want Father Dominic to see that he had started to cry.

Thomas choked back the tears as he gulped down half a carton of milk with the last of the hot dogs, hoping the food would push whatever was causing his sadness back down inside. It worked. As he felt the tears subside, he risked a quick glance at Father Dominic, finding him casually cutting a large section of tomato into smaller pieces. Thomas wondered what might be going through the priests' mind. As he gathered the courage to ask, Father Dominic got there first.

"So, tell me, Thomas, if you aren't sure about your belief in God, then what is it you do believe in?"

Thomas thought about how best to answer the question and then realized there probably wasn't a right answer out there. Like the prayer he had just said, Father Dominic would probably see beyond the words anyway. Perhaps it would be best to just be honest.

"I really don't know what I believe," he began, struggling to put into words what he had never admitted, even to himself. "I mean…like…for instance, the other day, I was in the shower thinking about all the water we use," he paused once more, squinting his eyes as if trying to see through fog. "And, you know, how some people don't have the same stuff. Like some kids in Africa can't just go to the bathroom and turn on a shower. I mean, like they have to walk for hours to get water! And, well, here I am, just turning a handle, and 'whoosh'!" He paused again, the puzzle pieces of his random thoughts beginning to form a picture.

"And, well, I'm standing there, and I'm thinking, like why would there be a God who would give some people instant water, and other people, like those kids in Africa, don't have what I do? It just didn't seem fair. And that led me to wonder…if God doesn't make these decisions, then who does? If he wasn't in charge, then who was? Like, where did our planet come from…and all the other planets…and the millions of other galaxies and stuff. I just don't get it. I mean, it seems like that's an awful waste of space and stuff for just one little planet of people.

But even if He did create the world, and everything else, well, why? Why did He need us in the first place? And what did He make all this stuff from? What was even here before He made everything? And where was He before there was all this for Him to be? And then…I was just standing there…for like, I don't know, but a long time. Just standing there thinking 'whoa'. You know what I'm trying to say?"

Father Dominic chuckled softly.

"That's quite the realization you had there. Most people go through life without even realizing what you just shared. Sure, they look up at the stars and wonder what it's all for, but I think your wonder went much deeper than that. You see, in that moment of awe, or 'whoa', as you called it, you found God, Thomas. In that moment, in the space between spaces, in the wonder of everything He's made, that's where we find Him. Jesus tells us, *"Behold, the Kingdom of God is in your midst."* I think you realized that in some way that day. You experienced the entirety of the whole Kingdom; looked through the eyes of God, if you will. But that doesn't fully answer the question. Given all that, what is it you believe?"

Thomas thought for a long moment, finishing off his second brownie and realizing he should have saved some of his milk. Shaking an empty container to indicate what he needed, he got up and walked to the soda fountain, coming back with two small glasses of root beer, and a couple of cookies, too. He sat down and started in on the first of the cookies, his eyes cast up towards the ceiling, deep in thought. As he quietly took small bites, he tried to organize his thoughts so they made sense. Failing that, he eventually just started talking again, letting the words once more find their own structure.

"I guess I believe there has to be a purpose for all this, somewhere. I mean, I read about how science has figured out how the universe started. Something about using these super powerful telescopes that look back in time or something so they can see images of light that existed at the moment of the Big Bang. And they can explain about evolution and all that. But no one has yet to explain why. I mean, there's probably a million billion ways the universe could have begun, but we're pretty sure the Big Bang is true. It's like, there was nothing, and then – boom – there's all this stuff. And I think, that kinda sounds like what it says in the Bible. You know, how God just says *'Let there be light'*, and – boom – there's all this light. So maybe science can help us understand how things happen. But for me, that's not enough. I guess I need to know *why* they happen. There's a part of me that believes that there is a God out there, or something else is, who knows what, but that doesn't matter, right? I mean, does it really matter if we call it God or Universal Mind like my philosophy teacher says, or even Pink Flamingo. It doesn't change what it is. I mean, a bird isn't a bird because we call it a bird. It doesn't matter what we call it. Every language calls it something a little different, and that doesn't mean that a bird changes what it is, right?"

Thomas felt strange sharing this, mostly because he had never talked like this before. He knew in the back of his mind he had considered these thoughts, but he had never put them into words before. Yet, here he was, his mouth barely keeping up with his brain as he continued.

"And maybe, just maybe, we aren't supposed to know. Not everything anyway. Maybe, part of human evolution involves our ability to understand what we see in different ways. Like, how many years did people think

# 26

the world was flat, and yet, it wasn't flat just because they thought it was, right? It wasn't like all of the sudden, someone thinks, '*Maybe the world is really round,*' and then – bam – it goes from flat to round over night! It was always round, but we just didn't see it like that. And maybe, just maybe, that's how it's supposed to be. Like with why some people have water whenever they want, and some people don't."

Thomas paused, becoming very comfortable with the words he was hearing himself share. Smiling slightly, he let his mind race on.

"Maybe we just haven't evolved to the point where we can understand why that is. We don't think about it because if you have water whenever you want, that's what you know. If you don't, then that's what you know. But if you take someone from America and put them in Africa and make them live a different lifestyle, well, then it would be different. Then it wouldn't feel right, and they might think about the world in a different way. Maybe we need to evolve into some new way of being human that allows us to understand God in a way that makes sense. Maybe someday we'll just look at things and think, '*Oh…that's what God wants from us.*' And I guess that's like believing in something without seeing it first. Isn't that what you said faith is all about? Believing in something before you see it for sure?"

Not waiting to see if Father Dominic agreed with him or not, Thomas continued.

"Well then, yeah…I guess that's what I believe."

He paused, glancing up at the ceiling again and then looking towards Father Dominic once more. Thomas' smile slowly stretched until it reached from ear to ear.

"Huh…" he said, "I never thought about it like that before. But yeah…I guess I do believe. I guess I really do have faith."

Thomas sat motionless, measuring the impact of the words he just heard himself admit for the first time ever. As he came to grips with the confession he had made – and in front of a priest no less – a small tear ran down his cheek. This time, however, the tear wasn't shed from sadness, or frustration, or turmoil, but from a place of complete and total peace. A feeling of overpowering joy began building up inside him as he sat there waiting for Father Dominic to respond. The world he thought he knew was falling apart, but he was happy. The entire house of cards that was his previous illusion of the world collapsed at his feet, and a new world of realization came into being. With barely a word, Father Dominic had led him to the greatest revelation of his life. He felt like a completely different person. Not just a person with a new set of beliefs, but a brand new human. With a warm, comfortable, joyful smile on his face, he watched as Father Dominic also shed a tear. For a moment, both men sat watching the other, silently crying great tears of joy. Eventually, Father Dominic broke the silence.

"And, with that, I do believe my work here is done," he joked playfully, drawing an even bigger smile from Thomas. "So, where do we go from here?"

Thomas didn't need but a moment to respond. As if he had planned this specific moment in time years before, he blurted out, "Tell me how to become a priest."

# Chapter Three
## The Winding Path

Thomas couldn't wait to get home. For the entire two-hour ride he visualized the conversations he thought would take place, imagining how thrilled his parents would be to hear his news. He saw his parents sitting on the edge of their seats as he announced his decision to enter the Seminary after he graduated from high school, which was just under three years away. On the movie screen of his mind, he saw his mom fall to her knees crying tears of joy, his dad rushing to him, giving him a hug so hard it nearly crushed his spine. He saw them pulling out their cell phones, updating their Facebook status with the news, calling relatives to brag, and taking selfies with him to capture the moment. He saw his mom in the kitchen making him his favorite dinner to celebrate, while Thomas sat with his dad at the kitchen table answering question after question about the experiences he had.

When the bus finally pulled into the parking lot at church, he could hardly contain his excitement. He saw a sea of cars and a crowd of parents, but he couldn't pick out the family car, nor find his parents. The bus came to a stop and the driver opened the doors. Thomas continued staring out the window, looking for any sign of his mom or dad, but there were too many people moving around. They were somewhere out there, he knew they were. As his turn to exit the bus came, he thought he caught a glimpse of his mom, but realized it wasn't her. He shrugged, pretending not to be concerned.

*"They're probably just running late,"* he thought. *"Maybe the bus got back early or something."*

Thomas grabbed his sleeping bag and luggage from the side of the bus and began to walk around the parking lot. Around him, the other teens were smiling, hugging parents or siblings, or stopping to take 'one last selfie' with a new friend they had met on the retreat. Suddenly, Thomas began to worry. This wasn't like his folks. They were usually the first ones to arrive on Sunday nights after Youth Group.

He found a place on the curb out of the way and waited. As each new car entered the lot, his hopes rose for a moment, only to drop back down when he saw it wasn't his folks. One after another the teens were picked up, waving a last goodbye to those that remained in the lot. Thomas watched them drive away, feeling more and more anxious. Between the distractions of vehicles coming and going back out, he stared at the pavement around his feet, his head hung low. A few times one of the other teens would call out his name, waving goodbye, or thanking him for being a part of the retreat. He would smile and wave back, trying to hold on to the high he had felt since his lunch with Father Dominic on Saturday. But that was fading fast. Sensing the presence of someone approaching, he looked up to see Amanda standing beside him. She had a curious look on her face.

"Hey, Thomas, how's it going?" she asked, obviously trying to seem casual.

"I'm good," he replied.

There was an awkward pause.

"So, I got a call on the way back from the retreat. You're probably wondering why your folks aren't here, right?" she went on, in an overly cautious manner.

Thomas shrugged, trying to pretend he wasn't wondering, or worried.

"Well," she paused, the word sounding hollow, "let's go into my office and chat, okay?"

Thomas noticed the seriousness in Amanda's voice, turning his head to look at her once more.

"Why?" he probed. "Something wrong?"

Amanda paused again, turning her head away. Was that a tear Thomas saw flicker in her eye as she turned? He wasn't sure he wanted to find out.

"Come on," she said. "I'll explain on the way."

Thomas stood up and grabbed his luggage. Amanda had already picked up his sleeping bag. Together they turned towards the school building where her office was, walking side by side. After a few steps, Amanda spoke to him; quietly, gently.

"There's just no easy way around this I guess. Your mom's in the hospital."

Thomas' feet stopped moving, his mind suddenly so rigidly trapped between wanting to know what happened and being afraid to find out that he could no longer control his own body. His thoughts raced faster than his words could keep up.

"What? How? Is she okay? What happened?" he blurted out rapidly, not waiting for a response.

"I can only tell you what I know," Amanda said slowly, deliberately.

Thomas felt like she was talking in slow motion. He was growing desperate, anxious. Just like he had yesterday morning on the retreat. Finally, she continued.

"Your parents had a fight. I don't know much about it. Just that it got out of hand, and your mom got hurt. The police officer who called me wouldn't tell me much. He got my cell phone number from your dad. He just asked me to find you and make sure you were okay. That's all I know right now," Amanda paused again, waiting to see how he might respond.

Thomas was deep in thought. A part of him wasn't surprised at the news. Behind the almost sickly sweet public version of his parents, there was a dark truth that only Thomas and his younger sister, Julianna, knew. Mom and Dad were not the best of friends.

The arguments had started about the time Thomas was in fourth or fifth grade, he couldn't remember. He never knew what set them off. One day they just started arguing; about money, about how much time Dad spent away from home, or about how Mom felt like she was doing everything around the house.

Eventually, the fights became more and more heated, but he had never seen them get physical. They had never even threatened each other before. They would yell, point fingers, curse, call each other wicked names, but never once did they lash out physically, at each other or at anything around them. Although Thomas had to admit, he never stuck around to watch. As soon as their arguments would start, he would head into his room, throw on his earphones, and drown out the noise however he could. Eventually, his little sister would come into his room, curl up against him, and wrap her arm around his chest. He would comfort her as best he could, at times sharing one of his earphones with her so she could listen in. Sometimes, especially if the fighting started later at night, they would fall asleep like that.

*His sister!*

"Julianna? Where is she? Was she there?" Thomas begged, dreading what the answer might be.

Amanda shook her head. "No. She was spending the weekend with a friend. She's still at that girl's house."

Thomas felt a slight sense of relief. Julianna was three years younger than he was and in the sixth grade. In many ways, she was still a child that played with dolls, had sleep-over parties, and always wanted Thomas to play dress-up or make-believe games. She was always the princess, and he was her prince. Lately, he had started pushing her away, saying he was 'too old' to play. Deep inside, he really did have fun the few times her persistent requests convinced him to participate. Not that he would ever admit it to her, or anyone else. A feeling of regret came over him for all those times he had said 'no,' wishing he could have them all back again.

"So, what now?" he asked, his emotions taking over. "What do I do? Can I go see my mom?"

Amanda shrugged her shoulders, obviously upset that she didn't have more information to share.

"I really don't know, Thomas. All I know is that there is someone coming over from the county sheriff's office to talk to you. They asked me to keep you here until they arrive. Come on, let's get inside where we can sit down," Amanda replied.

Thomas was deep in thought. He was glad Amanda wasn't saying anything. He needed this time to think. For the past few years, he had thought about running away, just leaving everything behind. Maybe that's why he had felt such a strong urge to do just that during the retreat. Maybe what had challenged him on Saturday morning was just his own fears boiling over. Father Dominic had said it was the Devil, but now, Thomas wasn't so sure. He still couldn't figure out why the Devil would be after him, or why he would care at all.

His mind drifted back to the conversation after lunch, barely twenty-four hours ago now. Father Dominic had asked him how serious he was to follow through on his question about becoming a priest, which, at the time, Thomas had felt there was nothing more he wanted. He didn't show his enthusiasm, though, much like he never showed Julianna how much he enjoyed being her prince. He thought it made him look soft-hearted to show his emotions. The last thing he ever wanted was to look weak.

It had been during that conversation when Father Dominic had told him, *"Well, if the Devil wants you this bad now, there's no telling what he might do to stop you from becoming a priest."*

Father Dominic had gone on to tell him about a few saints who had been challenged in similar ways by the Devil, like St. John Vianney, St. Padre Pio, and St. Gemma Galgani. Thomas had listened politely, still not convinced that any such 'demon' existed.

Suddenly, Thomas remembered something else Father Dominic had said. As the words came to him, he began to shiver, as if a freezing wind had just blown past.

*"When I say you should be always on your guard, Thomas, I don't mean just for another episode like the one you experienced here today. No, no. If the Devil is against you now, if it is his desire to turn you from your path, he won't only send his demons to strike at your heart. He will come at you from every way possible. He'll turn you against your friends, and them against you. Even your family won't be safe."*

Those last six words rang out again and again in Thomas' mind.

*"Even your family won't be safe."*

Could all of this be just as Father Dominic had predicted? Could the Devil have orchestrated the fight his parents had? Was it the Devil who sent his father into a rage so uncontrollable it ended with his mom getting hurt? Thomas suddenly felt frightened. He had never been in Amanda's office before. As he looked around trying to find what he needed, his first thought was how large it was. She had two refrigerators, three couches that were set in a U shape with a large table in the middle, a foosball table, and multiple bookcases filled with Bibles and copies of the Catechism, in both the regular version and the YouCat, a version written just for teens. A large collection of videos, both in DVD and the old VHS format, filled another bookshelf.

The walls were covered in t-shirts representing previous retreats, mixed in with dozens of pictures, and at least that many crosses, most of which were obviously handmade. There was a small shelf attached to one wall with a host of votive candles of every height, several variations of the crucifix, a statue of Our Lady of Guadalupe and one of the Blessed Mother and Child, along with several other religious items. Finally, tucked ever so simply in the back corner of the room, by far the smallest piece of furniture, Thomas saw Amanda's desk.

Somewhere, he knew, she would have what he needed. Father Dominic had given him instructions at lunch, teaching him a simple method to help protect him from any demonic attack. At the time, he had listened casually, not really believing he would ever be in need. Now, as the panic began to boil inside, he searched his memory for enough pieces from that conversation to remember what to do. He could already feel the darkness beginning to grow.

Thomas turned to Amanda. "I need your help. I need one of your candles and a rosary. We need to pray!"

The look on Amanda's face perfectly displayed her immediate thoughts. Thomas knew he was never the one to pray at Youth Group. Heck, he was barely involved in the games they did. He understood that this request probably came as somewhat of a shock to her, and so he extended his request once more.

"Please, Amanda, this is important," he pleaded. "We need to pray the rosary and I can't remember it all. You have to help me!"

Amanda nearly jumped, shocked at the urgency in his voice. Nodding her head, she leaped into action. "Yes, of course. Let me get what we need."

She gathered two rosaries with one hand, simultaneously reaching for a small picture with the other. The picture had an image of Jesus with two rays of light, one red and one white, shining out from his heart. JESUS, I TRUST IN YOU was written underneath in all caps. She grabbed one of the larger votive candles from the shelf and spent just a moment fishing through a drawer in her desk to find a box of matches. Having the supplies she required, Amanda pulled a small table between two of the couches and set everything up. When it was ready, she took a seat on one couch, motioning for Thomas to sit on the opposite side.

As they were about to begin, she jumped up once more, retrieving a small, metal plaque from behind her desk. On the front was a cartoon of a woman in a superhero outfit, complete with cape, kneeling before a cross. Above that, the inscription read:

*Prayer Powers, Activate!*

Amanda hung the sign on a small nail on the front of the door to her office and then closed the door softly.

"No one should bother us now," she said. "Everyone knows when that sign is up it means I'm in prayer. Is there anything specific you want to pray for?"

"Just for safety, for me and my family. And healing for my mom," Thomas replied.

They each made the sign of the cross and then began to pray. About thirty minutes later, as Amanda was putting everything away, a soft knock came on the door. Thomas looked up nervously. The top half of the door was mostly a window. Through the glass, Thomas saw a woman he had seen around the church before but had never met. Amanda also looked over, waving her in.

"Sorry to disturb you, Amanda," the woman began, "but there is a sheriff here, along with someone from Child Services?"

Amanda nodded. "Ah, yes. Please send them in. Thanks, Donna."

Donna turned and walked back down the hallway, the heels of her shoes clicking audibly on the tile floors. Thomas could make out just a few words of her hushed conversation with the visitors, then it was quiet once more. He began to fidget nervously. Eventually, he heard the sound of footsteps again on the tile hallway, this time he could tell it was a larger group. He didn't know what to expect from this encounter, or what it might mean for himself or his family. He also wished Father Dominic had come back with the bus, and that he was sitting beside him right now.

Donna returned, entering the room just far enough to usher two visitors inside. A woman entered first, followed by a very tall and imposing man in the uniform of the County Sheriff. The two visitors walked in just far enough for Donna to close the door behind them as she left. Thomas listened once more to the clicking sounds her shoes made as she returned to her desk, secretly wishing he could have followed her out of the room.

Amanda had finished putting away the prayer items and was sitting at her desk, writing furiously on a piece of paper. She turned to the two adults, who were still standing at the door, and motioned them to take seats at one of the couches. The woman sat down on the left side of Thomas, while the sheriff made his way over to the couch on his right. Amanda returned to where she had been sitting across from Thomas, and then handed the paper she had been working on to the sheriff. Thomas wanted to be anywhere but in this room right now. He looked to Amanda, hoping she would sense his nervousness, but she just smiled back.

"Hello, Thomas," the woman sitting next to him said. "I'm Maureen, from the Office of Social Services. And this," she said, waving her hand towards the officer, "is Sheriff William Dunn. I believe by now Amanda told you why we are here?"

Thomas just nodded his head.

"Well, then. First let me tell you, your mom is going to be okay. She will probably come home in a few days, from what the doctors told me. Oh, I should have asked," she paused a moment, glancing towards Amanda, then back to Thomas. "Do you want us to be alone? Or are you okay with Amanda being here?"

Thomas looked at Amanda. He didn't think it mattered one way or the other, but since the last thing he wanted was to be outnumbered, he replied, "Yeah…she can stay, I guess."

Maureen smiled at him, then looked at Officer Dunn for acknowledgment. He simply nodded his agreement, his face firm and expressionless.

"Okay. Good. So tell me what you already know so far?" Maureen asked.

"Not much," Thomas replied. "Just something about my parents getting into a fight or something? And Mom getting hurt. What happened? Where's my dad?"

Officer Dunn was the one to respond. "He's down at the station now. We're holding him while we complete our investigation of the situation. He might have to stay there, at least overnight, until a judge reviews the case."

*"Wow,"* Thomas thought, *"this is more serious than I thought. Dad...in jail?"*

He looked from Officer Dunn to Maureen, to Amanda, and back, hoping someone would just tell him what happened.

"We don't know what started the fight. Your dad says it started like any one of their fights normally start," Maureen began, pausing just a moment before asking, "How often did you see them argue?"

Thomas shrugged, "I dunno... I guess a couple times a month?"

"Did your dad ever hit your mom before?" Officer Dunn inquired.

Thomas shook his head.

"Ever threaten her? Or hit anyone else?"

Again, Thomas shook his head, starting to feel uncomfortable with the way Officer Dunn spoke to him.

"You're sure? You're not just saying this to protect him or anything, are you?"

Thomas glared at Officer Dunn. He didn't like what he was hearing.

"My dad's a good guy. I don't know what happened, or why, but he never hit anyone that I saw. Not no one," Thomas blurted out, a bit angrily.

"Okay, son…okay. I'm sorry, but I gotta ask. I'm sure your dad is a decent enough guy. Just got out of hand last night. That can happen. But I gotta ask my questions. Just be honest with your answers, and we'll get through this just fine, okay?" Officer Dunn stated.

After a moment's consideration, Thomas nodded.

Maureen took over the conversation. "Thomas, I know this is hard stuff to deal with at your age. But you have to trust us. We're here to help the situation. We need to make sure you and your sister… and your mom…are going to be safe. We don't want to let your dad back in the house if this might happen again, okay?"

Thomas had been looking at her while she said this, watching her eyes, trying to decide if he could trust her or not. She seemed nice enough, he decided, although he still wasn't sure about Officer Dunn. He considered his options, turning his gaze to the carpet at his feet. Realizing it was probably best to cooperate, he nodded softly, not looking up from the ground.

"Okay, good," Officer Dunn went on, "So you ain't seen him do nothing like this before, huh? Never even threatened you or your mom? Or your sister? A neighbor maybe?"

Thomas shook his head, still not looking up.

"Well, that's good I guess. Any idea what might have set him off this time?" he inquired.

Thomas looked up, holding Officer Dunn's gaze.

"I dunno. They argued a lot I guess. Dad almost always got mad when Mom spent more money than she was supposed to. Mom always got mad when Dad said he had to travel for work. I didn't pay much attention to them. That's just what they did. I was pretty sick of it since you want the truth."

Officer Dunn smirked, looking at Thomas for a moment longer, then nodded to Maureen.

"So, I guess you want to know what's next for you, right?" she asked.

Thomas nodded.

"Well, we can't send you home. You're just, how old now, thirteen?"

"I'm gonna be sixteen next month! I'm not some little kid! I can take care of myself!" Thomas exclaimed.

"Oh, I'm sure you can, Thomas. But you see, the state won't allow that. I know you probably don't understand it at your age, but there are rules we need to follow in situations like this. We just can't let a minor go without supervision. And we probably need to find someone to take you to see your mom. You do want to see your mom, right?"

Thomas felt trapped. It felt like she just said that if he didn't cooperate, then they wouldn't take him to see his mom. Were they really holding that over his head? Or was that just his imagination? Again, he felt like he had no choice but to agree.

"Yeah, of course, I do," Thomas said, feeling a deep sense of despair creeping in.

"Well, then, we have one option that might work," Maureen began, looking at Amanda. "Luckily there are a few foster homes in our system with people from your church. Amanda provided us with a couple of names, houses that are open to having kids come stay with them in situations like this. We've got one couple waiting right now to come down and pick you up."

She paused for a moment, waiting for Thomas to respond. When he didn't, she continued. "Unless you have a relative close by or something?"

Thomas knew his closest relative was at least a six-hour drive from where he lived.

"Why can't I just go stay with one of my friends, like my sister is doing?" he asked.

"That's where things get tricky," Maureen began. "You see, when this situation happened, Julianna was already at her friend's house, so she has permission to be there until one of your parents picks her up. But, up until about an hour ago, you only had permission to be away from the house until the end of the retreat. Technically, Amanda is responsible for you right now, but she can't take you home with her, because of church restrictions and all that. With your dad in custody, and with your mom in surgery right now..." her voice trailed off.

Thomas interrupted, shouting, "Surgery! I thought you said she was okay! What the hell happened?"

"Calm down, son," Officer Dunn demanded with a strong authoritarian tone.

Thomas glared at him. He didn't like being called 'son' so often. He didn't know this guy, and, frankly, he didn't care if he was an officer or not. He thought the man was rude.

"Thomas, please. Look at me," Amanda said in a soft, pleading voice.

Thomas turned his gaze to Amanda, realizing in that moment that he had stood up when he shouted. She reached up and took his hands, holding them firmly as she looked into his eyes. He collapsed back into the couch, sinking deeply into the cushions. He wished he could sink all the way down into nothing.

"We're all doing the best we can in this situation," Amanda said. "There's only so much we can share with you, because of your age and all. But yes, she's in surgery right now. Now, the doctors have said she's going to be okay. And she should come home soon. We just need to figure out where you're going to stay for a few nights."

She paused. After a moment, Thomas raised his eyes and looked into hers.

"Trust me," she continued. "I know the Thompson family. They're good people. You've probably seen them around. They have a daughter a couple years older than you. She's helped out a few times with Youth Group. Her name's Lily. She's tall; has long red hair; and she's always wearing those sheepskin boots, even in the summer. Ring any bells?"

Thomas thought about it, then shook his head.

"And they'll take me to see my mom? Can my mom tell me what happened? I'm not some dumb kid. I can handle it," he said.

"Yes. I promise you. They'll take you tonight. As soon as your mom is out of surgery. And yes, if your mom wants to tell you, she can say anything she wants to. She's your mom. It's her right to decide how much you know or don't know right now," Amanda told him, her voice wavering just slightly as she spoke.

Maureen put her hand on his shoulder. "It's going to be fine, Thomas. It's all going to be okay. I've seen situations like this before. Your mom will come home soon. And when she does, she's going to need you there to help her out. I don't know what she's going to do about your dad, if they'll work it out, or if she'll ask him to move out. Either way, she's going to need you to help out for a while. She's going to need you to be strong, okay?"

Thomas nodded one more time. There was a pause in the room. Not awkward, but noticeable. Officer Dunn finally broke the silence.

"Well, then. I guess we're done here. You got the Thompson's coming to pick him up soon?" he asked Amanda.

Now it was her turn to nod. "Yeah. They said they could be here within the hour. Okay if he stays with me until they get here?"

Officer Dunn looked at Maureen. Seeing that she agreed, he said, "Sure. That's fine. And thanks for your help here, Amanda. Please keep us informed if you think either of us needs to step back in, okay?"

"Oh, trust me, Bill. I'll keep my eye on this one," Amanda said.

Amanda walked Maureen and Officer Dunn to the door, shaking their hands and thanking them for their help. She took something from Maureen, waved goodbye once more, and closed the door. Coming back to the couch where Thomas was sitting, she held the item Maureen had given her to him. Thomas saw it was a business card with Maureen's name and number on it, along with a few emergency phone numbers; the police, a domestic violence hotline, and a suicide prevention hotline. Thomas looked it over, deciding there was one phone number that wasn't on the card – one he felt he would need.

"Amanda?" he said sheepishly. "There's one number missing here. Well, two actually."

"Oh yeah? Which two are those?" she smiled at him, knowing what he was about to ask.

"Well, yours, of course," he replied. "And one for Father Dominic, too."

Amanda held out her hand. "Let me see that."

Thomas handed her the card, watching as she carried it over to her desk, grabbed a pen, and scribbled a few things down. She came back and handed it to him triumphantly.

"That better?" she asked.

Thomas looked it over. "Yeah, that should do."

"Just no calls at two in the morning unless it's an emergency. Got it?" she requested, gently smiling.

"Yeah, I got it," he agreed.

"I'm going to go talk to Donna for a moment. Help yourself to whatever you find in the fridge," Amanda stated as she turned towards the door, pausing just before she left the room to take one last look back his way.

Thomas waited until her footsteps could no longer be heard down the hall, then got up and rummaged through the refrigerator, grabbing a generic version of Mountain Dew. Next to the fridge, he found a box filled with lunchbox-sized snacks. He picked up two bags of Cheetos and walked over to the foosball table. Looking for something to take his thoughts from worrying about his mom, he did his best to play a solo game.

Eventually, Amanda came back in and asked if he wanted a foosball partner or not. Thomas shook his head. He tossed the empty Cheetos bags in the trash and sat back down on the couch.

"I wish Father Dominic was here," he admitted.

"You two really hit it off on the retreat, huh?"

"Yeah, I guess," Thomas said, absent-mindedly picking at something sticky on his jeans. "Any idea where he is now?"

"By now, unless he stopped for food, or caffeine, more likely," she chuckled, glancing at her watch, "he's probably halfway back to L.A. That's where he's from."

"Really?" Thomas considered, then asked, "What made him come all the way up here? That's like, what, a ten-hour drive?"

"More like eight, maybe nine, depending on traffic," Amanda informed him, adding, "He used to be assigned to this parish, way back when I was a teen. That's how I know him. He was the Youth Pastor back then, and we've been friends ever since. He actually helped me get this job. He's a really good guy, Thomas. One of the best I've known. Not every priest can hang with you crazy teens. You're lucky he took you under his wing like that. It means you're special."

Thomas didn't feel very special, especially with everything that was going on in his life right now.

"So...what did you two talk about yesterday?" Amanda inquired.

Thomas wondered how much he should share with her. It wasn't that he didn't trust Amanda. She seemed to genuinely care, and he felt comfortable around her. It was just that he hadn't reached a decision yet as to what it all meant. Truthfully, though, he didn't have anything to lose at this point. And so, he shared the story of what happened on Saturday morning and most of his conversation with Father Dominic at lunch. Amanda listened attentively, holding any questions she might have until he was done. When he finished, they sat in silence for a time.

"That's quite the experience, Thomas," Amanda began. "What do you think it all means?"

Thomas thought about it, his eyes closing slightly.

"Honestly, I don't know. I mean, Father Dominic says the dark feeling I felt was the Devil and that he probably wants to turn me from some path I'm supposedly on. But I don't know about all that. I mean, like earlier when you said I must be special, that's the same thing Father Dominic said. But I guess, well, I guess I never considered myself any different or nothing. I sure don't feel special right now, that's for sure."

Amanda sat quietly, her eyes fixed on Thomas. Eventually, she shifted her position slightly.

"We never really know what it is God has planned for us, Thomas. But let me ask you this. Do you believe you were born for a purpose?" she inquired, her eyes holding his. "Do you believe there is something God meant for you to do when He created you?"

Thomas nodded his head.

"I guess so. I mean, like I told Father Dominic, I don't think life is just some random event. I believe there is something behind all this. I just wish I knew what."

"I know what you mean. I was in a similar place when I was a little older than you. Not with the situation with your parents and all, but in trying to decide what God wanted from me. Can I share my story with you?" Amanda asked.

"Yeah, sure."

"Well, I really didn't know what I was going to do after high school. I went on my Confirmation Retreat as a junior, and it was in the spring, so I only had about a year to decide. On that retreat, I went to reconciliation with Father Dominic, and we really hit it off, just like the two of you did. I shared with him my concerns about life, and he said something that really stuck with me. He asked me one question, then said he didn't want an answer right away. He told me to think about it, pray about it, and to dedicate a rosary every morning to my patron saint. I asked him who my patron saint might be, and he told me it would become clear when the time was right. Until it was clear, I was to keep praying rosaries to whomever my patron saint might be.

"I did that for a month, maybe a little more. Then one night, I had a vision. At least, that's what I'm calling it. I had a dream anyway, with St. Gemma Galgani. She's also known as the Gem of Christ, and the Lily of Lucca. Anyway, she was only twenty-five when she died, but she had already experienced visions of her own for eighteen years by then. She is my favorite of all the saints.

"In the dream, St. Gemma told me her greatest concern, that the youth of our world aren't finding Christ the way she did in her youth. She asked me to be his advocate to the youth. I didn't know what that meant, but that next morning, I got a call from Father Dominic, asking me if I had come up with an answer to the question he had asked me on that retreat."

Thomas interrupted, "What was the question? You never said what he asked you."

Amanda smiled.

"Oh, I was getting to that. His question was a simple one, but it took me that whole month to come up with an answer. He asked me to explain the mystery of salt."

Thomas snorted.

"Exactly! That's what I thought, too! But after putting some thought into it, I came across a definition that stuck, and one that has been with me ever since. It's helped mold my life into what it is today. You see, salt, in and of itself, really isn't much. It's just a chemical compound. Sure, you can cook with it, or cure olives, or even clean with it. But that's just it…you need that 'something else' in order for salt to find its purpose. Without that 'something else', it's just 'salt'," Amanda explained, pausing to give Thomas time to consider what she had said.

"Look at how it's used in food, for example. Let's say you got a nice hot order of fries at In-n-Out, and they forgot to salt them. How would they taste?" she asked Thomas.

"Pretty bland I guess," he replied.

"Exactly. But when you add the salt, it draws out the flavors of the fries, makes them more enjoyable. And there is only one way that the salt can do that," she continued.

"How's that?" Thomas asked, becoming very interested in the conversation.

"By surrendering what it is. For it to work, salt must dissolve. It must become nothing, allow everything that it is to be absorbed by the fries. It must penetrate the essence of 'fries'. Only then does the mystery work," she explained.

"Oh, I get it. It's like if the salt didn't dissolve into the food, then some of the food might still taste bland, and some of it might be too salty," Thomas offered.

Amanda smiled, nodding her head.

"No wonder Father Dominic liked you so much. You're a pretty quick thinker," Amanda said, smiling broadly. "So, using this analogy of salt, I realized that's what I wanted to do with my life. I wanted to be salt for other people, to find ways to flavor their day, to help them move from a bland, meaningless life, to a new way of thinking. The best way I could think of to do that was through ministry. Oh, I'm sure I could find ways to be that type of person in any job I took, but to be salt for the whole world, I knew I had to dedicate myself to ministry. Suddenly, my world opened up. I knew exactly what it was that God wanted me to do, and exactly why Saint Gemma was the one who visited me that night.

"From that point on, I became the person my friends turned to for support. I helped them understand problems they were dealing with, helped them get through relationships, deal with their parents…you know, typical teenage stuff. And it just grew from there. I started helping out here at Youth Group, became a member of the Ministry Team during college, and, well, one thing led to another. Eventually, Father Dominic offered me the job of Youth Minister. I've been doing that for over five years now, and I couldn't imagine myself doing anything other than this," Amanda shared.

"I think the same holds true for you, Thomas. I think Father Dominic saw something in you, something you may never have seen for yourself, like he did with me. I'll bet if you hadn't told him that day you wanted to be a priest, he would have asked you to tell him the mystery of salt! But you jumped the gun. Like I said, you're a pretty quick thinker."

Once more the sound of heels clicking on tile was heard. Amanda stood up, holding her hand.

"Come with me. That's probably Donna coming to say that Mr. and Mrs. Thompson are here," she said.

Together, arm in arm, they walked out of her office. Thomas still felt his fears and doubts about the future lingering in the background, but they weren't as prevalent now. He knew he had someone he could reach out to when he needed, someone who would make sacrifices to help him through what he was experiencing. And for now, that was all he could ask for.

# CHAPTER FOUR
## CONSIDER THE LILY

Outside, Amanda introduced Thomas to Ben and Terri Thompson. They took turns telling him how sorry they were for what he was going through, and promising him they would do everything they could to make his situation easier. Ben went with Amanda to her office to retrieve Thomas' luggage, while Terri followed Donna into the rectory office to complete a few forms, leaving Thomas by himself for the first time since he had learned about his mom. He sat back down on the curb, lost in thought. For the fourth time in the past two days, he decided to pray.

"God, I don't know if you're listening, but I'm going to believe that you are. Or at least that my patron saint is, if I have one. I don't know what you want from me right now, or why this is happening, but I'm going to trust you. I'm going to trust that the Thompson's are good people. I'm going to trust that my mom has the best doctors and that she's going to be fine. I'm going to trust that my dad is going to be good as well. I'll do anything you ask me to for all of this to turn out. I don't care about me, I just want my family to be okay. I mean it, whatever you want from me, I'll do it. Just tell me what it is, please."

He pushed back the tears as emotions once more overwhelmed him. He suddenly realized he had prayed, and cried, more on this retreat weekend than he had in years. He never thought he could feel so much emotion at once, never realized he cared as deeply as he did about the life he had, or the parents that raised him. Maybe this tragedy with his parents was just what he needed to realize what truly mattered in life. Maybe it was a way of waking up to the reality of his world.

He rubbed at his eyes with the palms of his hands, wiping away the evidence of his emotional display, then turned at the sound of Mr. Thompson coming back out with his luggage.

"I can help you with that, Mr. Thompson," he said.

"First thing you can do to help, is to stop calling me 'Mr. Thompson'. The name's Ben. I'm more comfortable with you calling me that, okay?" Ben responded.

"Sure, I guess," Thomas replied.

Ben handed him his sleeping bag and opened the trunk. He placed the luggage in first, then stepped aside to allow Thomas to load his bag in.

"By the way," Ben shared, "Mrs. Thompson would rather you call her Terri. We both grew up regular farm people, not a lot of need for formality in our house. So, just Ben and Terri is fine."

Thomas nodded, slipping into the back seat of the car as Terri came out of the office.

"Good to go?" Ben asked.

"Yeah. We're good," Terri replied.

Ben got in and started the car as Terri walked around to the other side. As she was buckling her seatbelt, Amanda came out of the office to wave them off.

"Hold on," Thomas pleaded, "I'll be right back!"

He leaped from the car, racing to where Amanda stood, and threw his arms around her neck. After a few seconds of shock at his gesture, she returned his hug. The moment lasted no more than a minute or two, but the impact was one Thomas would feel for the rest of his life.

"Thank you, Amanda. I really appreciate everything you're doing for me. I promise I will repay you someday," Thomas said.

"No need for promises, Thomas. Just go be the best person you can right now. Your family is going to need someone to help tie everything back together. Can you do that for me?" Amanda asked.

Thomas leaned back, slightly separating their hug. He looked at Amanda for a long moment, his eyes locked on hers, wondering if he was strong enough.

"Yeah...I think I can do that."

"Good. Then the only promise I will accept from you is that you'll promise to call me if you ever need. It's going to be tough for a bit, but not forever. You have to remember that, okay?" Amanda squeezed his arms as they broke apart.

Thomas nodded, smiling back at her. Then he turned and got into the car. A minute or so later, they were turning out of the parking lot, heading towards his new, temporary home.

"Ben?" Thomas said.

"Yeah, Thomas?"

"I know you said you wanted to take me to your house first, but I really would like to go see my mom. Please," Thomas begged.

Terri turned in her chair so she was facing him.

"I know Thomas, and we will, I promise. It's just, well, we can't get into your house to pick up any of your things right now, so we aren't sure what you might need. We thought, if we can just stop by the house, which is on the way anyhow, we can make a quick list of what you need, and you can get cleaned up. Then Ben can drive you to the hospital while Lily and I go shopping. Okay?"

Thomas thought about it.

"Why can't we get into my house?" he inquired.

"Well, the police still have it taped off, being that it's a crime scene and all that. Plus, I don't think you want to see it until it gets all cleaned up," Terri admitted.

"Cleaned up? From what?" he demanded.

"From…everything I guess," Terri started to explain, hesitating as she searched for the right words, "you know your mom got hurt pretty bad, right?"

"People keep saying that, but no one will tell me how bad. And I know, you guys can't say anything either, 'cause I'm not eighteen or whatever, and you're not my parents."

Thomas could feel his anger starting to creep back in. He knew the situation wasn't the Thompson's fault, but knowing that didn't help. With a sigh, he sunk back into his seat.

"Whatever. Do what you have to, just get me to my mom soon, okay?"

Terri looked like she was about to say something else, but, instead, simply turned back to face the front, glancing over at her husband as he drove. Thomas saw Ben reach over with his right hand, grasp his wife's left arm and the squeeze it gently. Feeling lost and despondent once more, Thomas pulled out his phone and checked the display. His battery was at nine percent. Definitely not enough to start playing music right now.

"I'm gonna need a charger," he announced. "My phone is just about dead."

"There should be one in the glove box. Terri, can you dig it out?" Ben asked. "Oh, and there's a place to plug it in on that console thing between the back seats. Just fold it down. You see it?"

Thomas looked to his right, saw what Ben was referring to, and pulled down a section of the middle seat. He took the USB cable that Terri handed to him and plugged it in, putting the other end in his phone. He decided not to use the phone right away so it could get as much charge as possible. He didn't know when the next time he would be able to charge it might be.

"We probably have a few extra of those at home, but we'll make sure to pick one up for you," Terri informed him, typing quickly on her own phone. "Anything else you can think of that you absolutely need for tonight? I mean, besides the usual stuff, like a toothbrush and all that. I already have that on my list. Do you need any medications? Or anything special we need to know?"

"Nothing I can think of. Although, I'm a bit hungry. Haven't eaten since breakfast, and it's like, what, three or something now?"

"A little past three actually. What do you feel like? We can pick something up on the way to the house," Ben suggested.

"Whatever. I'm not picky. Whatever is easiest. I don't have any cash on me, though," Thomas shared.

"No worries kid. We've got you covered while you're with us. Don't even think about it," Ben said.

Twenty minutes later, Thomas, face deep in a giant burrito, looked up as the sound of gravel crunching under the tires drew his attention. The Thompson's driveway wound between a series of tall Italian cypress trees, blocking most of his view. All he could see was a large, plain looking building, resembling more of a barn than a house. He remembered Ben saying something about growing up on a farm, but living inside a barn? That was a bit too much.

As Ben pulled up to the 'barn', one of the walls lifted up, allowing them to pull inside. Thomas realized this building, which was almost as large as the home he and his family lived in, wasn't the Thompson's house, but only the garage. A gigantic, oversized, five-car garage, complete with a second floor that looked like a small office. Thomas saw at least three desks, a conference table, and two separate offices with glass walls. As they got out, Ben noticed the look of awe on Thomas' face.

"This is where I hang out during the week. It's okay to come in if you need me for something, but this is where my employees and I work. I'll bring you down tomorrow morning to meet them, make sure you're comfortable and that they know who you are. After that, unless you really need anything, this area is pretty much off limits, at least during the working hours," Ben informed him.

"Okay. I won't disturb you," Thomas replied.

Ben walked around the back of the car and opened the trunk, pulling out the luggage and sleeping bag, saying, "You go on and follow Terri inside. I'll bring these in for you."

Thomas followed Terri to a door on the side of the garage. As they exited, he almost tripped over his own two feet. There before him was the most magnificent house he had ever seen. The front door had to be twenty feet tall, with enormous white pillars on each side that supported a large, second-floor balcony. In front of each pillar was an Italian Cypress, meticulously cut in spiral swirls. The front façade was almost all brick, from the ground to half-way up the second floor. Thomas figured there had to have been at least two dozen windows on the front. He wondered how many bedrooms there were.

As he followed Terri along a perfectly landscaped gravel path, decorated on each side with a wide variety of plants, Thomas began to feel embarrassed about his appearance. He absentmindedly brushed at whatever dirt might be on his shirt, forgetting that he still held a half-eaten burrito in his hand. He wiped the burrito twice down the front of his shirt before a large glob of refried beans landed with a 'plop' on the top of his shoe. He looked down at the mess in complete embarrassment.

"Oh, my God…I'm so sorry. I totally forgot I had that in my hand. Oh man…I really fu…uh, I mean, I really messed myself up."

Thomas was even more embarrassed now, having almost cursed in front of Terri. As anxiety flooded through him, he suddenly felt two feet tall. Terri grabbed his hand, the one without the burrito remnants, and looked him over.

"Well now." she giggled at him, trying to ease his embarrassment. "I can't take you in through the front door looking like that. Let's use the side entrance, it's right next to the laundry room. I might have something in there you can put on."

As they reached the side entrance door, she stopped him just short of the landing.

"Go ahead and kick off those shoes outside here. We're not neat freaks or anything, but I really don't want to be cleaning Taco Bell off all my floors," Terri said, laughing again, just loud enough for Thomas to feel like she was trying to make him feel better. It wasn't working.

Thomas felt even more embarrassed now. As he fought back the feelings, he thought back to the bus ride home from the retreat and the excitement he had felt about coming home. Now, here he was just two hours later, covered in burrito, and no one to share his news with. How fast his life had changed. Father Dominic might have been right about him being a target of the Devil after all. This much bad stuff just wasn't supposed to happen to one person all on the same day, let alone within two hours. He sighed audibly, watching as Terri came back down the hall carrying a bright yellow t-shirt and a pair of fuzzy slippers with giant monkey heads.

"Best I could do in a pinch, Thomas. I'll find you something better once we get you upstairs. Go ahead and take off that shirt while you're still outside, and, by the looks of it, those socks have had better days as well."

Thomas looked again at his feet. His socks were filthy. Though, that made sense since he had just come back from a retreat in the woods. It was a wonder there was anything about him that was clean. Suddenly he didn't feel at all ready to enter into this mansion. Now that he thought of it, maybe his whole body was just as dirty. Feeling extremely self-conscious, uncomfortable, and more than a bit nauseous, he turned away from Terri.

"I apologize, Thomas, I should have realized you probably wanted a more private place to change. Let me see if the downstairs bathroom is available," she said, covering her eyes.

"No…no…that's okay. I was thinking about something else is all," Thomas said, quickly pulling off his stained shirt and replacing it with the bright yellow one. As he pulled it over his head, a wonderful scent infused his nostrils, and a warm feeling flushed over him. Terri reached out one hand, the other one still covering her eyes.

"Just hand everything to me and let me know when you're done," she said.

Thomas bundled everything, making sure the burrito mess was inside, then handed the bundle to Terri.

"Come on," Terri said, taking her hand away from her eyes and turning to lead Thomas into the house, "let's get you to your room."

Thomas followed her down a long, wide, tiled hallway, past doorway after doorway, through a huge kitchen, and down into what he figured must be a family room. The room was massive, with a pool table on one side, and the biggest flat screen TV he had ever seen along the opposite wall. The TV was on, currently playing an episode of The Fosters. With his attention on the TV, he didn't notice the person sitting on the couch.

As he and Terri turned a corner, a voice called out, "Well, well...don't you look cute!"

Thomas stopped in his tracks, looking over his shoulder to see where the voice had come from. By the description Amanda had given him earlier, the girl he was staring at now had to be Lily. She was one of the tallest girls he had ever seen, with long, bright red hair that blossomed over her shoulders. The only thought running through his mind was how absolutely beautiful she was. Thomas realized he was staring, feeling embarrassment once more. He looked around, thinking she must have been talking to someone else, but no one else was there.

"Yeah, you. That's a very pretty blouse you have on," Lily giggled, smiling from ear to ear.

Thomas looked down, noticing for the first time that the bright yellow t-shirt he had put on wasn't a t-shirt at all, but a girl's sweater, complete with a floral design on the left breast, just over his rapidly beating heart.

*"As if this day couldn't get any worse,"* Thomas thought.

Here he was, standing in front of one of the most beautiful girls he had ever met, wearing a woman's floral sweater, with two huge monkey head slippers smiling up at him.

"Lily, be nice!" Terri said. "The poor kid has had it pretty rough today. Tell you what, why don't you take him up to his room."

Lily giggled again. "Sure thing, Mom. I'll see if I can find one of Bobby's old shirts while we're up there."

She jumped off the couch, grabbing Thomas by the hand. In a mockingly formal voice, she said, "Come along princess, I believe it is time to change."

Pulling him along, Lily took him down yet another hallway, this one opening into a massive room with ceilings so high Thomas felt dizzy just looking up. In the center of the wall, he could see the inside of the front door, the windows on either side looking out at the spiral trees and meticulously manicured front yard. The entry opened up into three different hallways, the middle one they had just come down, and one on either side. Between the three hallways, a staircase spiraled up to a landing on the next floor.

"So much for being just farm people," Thomas whispered.

"What was that?" Lily asked, turning to face him.

Thomas felt his face start to burn.

"Oh, um, nothing. I was just thinking aloud, I guess," he mumbled, hoping she hadn't understood what he had said.

Lily gave him a curious glance, then winked and smiled, pulling him forward once more. She led him towards the stairs on the left. As they began to climb, Lily turned her head, looking over her shoulder.

"So, you know my name is Lily, what's yours again?" she asked.

"Thomas," came his terse reply, still feeling somewhat embarrassed, as well as a bit smitten.

"Well, I'm glad to meet you, Thomas. You from around here?"

"Yeah, just the other side of town, you know, where all us princesses come from."

Lily laughed at that, squeezing his hand as she did. Thomas didn't know why he had said that last part, but he was glad that he had. He liked the way Lily laughed. It was melodic, gentle and infectious.

"So…what they got ya in for, kid?" Lily inquired, changing her voice to sound raspy and rough.

"Just need a place to stay for a day or so I guess. My mom's in the hospital," he replied.

"Oh, man. I'm sorry to hear that. She okay?" Lily inquired, stopping once more to turn to him.

Thomas wasn't sure how much he was supposed to share, plus, he didn't want Lily to ask a bunch of questions when he still had so many questions of his own.

"Yeah, they say she'll be alright," he said quietly, hoping she wouldn't probe.

"Well, that's good then, I guess. Wait here."

She let go of his hand as she disappeared into a bedroom. Thomas glanced at his still warm hand. He lifted it slowly to his nose, pausing to breathe in the scent she left behind. His hand had the same smell as the sweater he was wearing, telling him the sweater most likely belonged to her. Smiling to himself, he rolled his hand into a ball, not wanting to let go of the warmth he had felt while it was holding hers. As he glanced down the hallway, Lily returned, triumphantly holding a faded black t-shirt. She held it up against his shoulders, looked him over, and then posed dramatically, one hand on her hip and the other hanging somewhat limply in the air.

"Dahling, this one is definitely you. Très chic!" she said in an exaggerated French accent.

"Uh…thanks?" Thomas responded, curious how he had never noticed her before at Youth Group.

Amanda had told him she volunteered there from time to time. He honestly thought, with a personality like this, let alone her stunning beauty, he would have noticed her by now.

When Thomas didn't respond any further, Lily dropped her arms quickly, gasping, "Ugh…men!"

She turned back down the hall, grabbed his hand once more, and dragged him along.

"Let's go, sport," she said.

They passed one more door before stopping at the next. Lily stood rigidly by the closed door, then bowed low, waving her left hand in quick circular motions in front of her face as she did.

"Monsieur," she said, again in her best French accent, "welcome to your new room."

She opened the door and waved him inside. Thomas looked in, not believing what he saw. It was larger than any bedroom he had been in before. On one wall was a queen size bed with two nightstands, one on each side. Along another wall, he saw a desk with a computer, writing pad, and a slew of organizers. On the third wall, he saw a long chest of drawers. Next to that, taller than he was, sat a full-size armoire. On the final wall, there was a big screen TV, though not as large as the one downstairs. Under the TV was a stand with every gaming console he could think of.

"Holy Jesus!" Thomas exclaimed.

"Yeah," Lily replied, "Pretty dope, huh?"

Thomas walked further in, noticing there were two doors, one on each of the walls next to the bed.

"Where do those go?" he asked.

Lily once again dropped into character, this time taking on the voice of a TV game show host. "Johnny, tell the lad what's behind door number one!"

As she spoke, she raced to stand by the door on the left of the bed. Changing her voice, she continued, "Well, Thomas! Behind door number one is your own…" she opened the door in dramatic fashion, "…walk-in closet!"

Lily then ran to the bed, half jumping, half sliding across, ending up at the second door.

"And behind door number two…your own bathroom!" Lily finished by making a sound like the roar of a crowd, then leaped once more back onto the bed, somersaulted, and ended up in a seated position with one leg tucked under her and the other draped over the side.

Thomas laughed. He needed this moment right now. He was holding so much emotion, so much worry for his mom and sister, and so many questions about his dad. He really just needed to laugh for a change.

"Thomas?" Lily asked.

"Yeah?" he replied.

"You ever gonna give me back my sweater? Or are you getting comfortable with your feminine side?" she said, smiling at him sheepishly.

"Oh, yeah. Sorry," he mumbled, heading off in the direction of the bathroom.

Again, as he entered, he was taken aback by the size and ornate features. There was even a TV and speakers in the shower! He pulled off the sweater, replacing it with the featureless, faded black t-shirt Lily had found for him. The shirt was much larger than he normally wore, with sleeves that drooped past his elbows. The bottom of the shirt hung almost to his knees. Thomas walked back out to the bedroom and handed the yellow sweater to Lily.

"I'll bet it smells like 'dude' now, huh?" she joked, putting it briefly to her nose, then pulling it away quickly. "Ewww…sorry, Thomas, but it does kinda stink."

Thomas realized he hadn't showered since Saturday morning, and the showers at the retreat hadn't been that effective either.

"Sorry. I haven't had time to clean up yet," he said, embarrassed for what felt like the hundredth time today.

"Where've you been?" she asked, testing the odor on the sweater once more. "It smells like smoke."

"Just got back from the retreat," he replied.

"Oh, man…that's right. That was this weekend. Campfire on Saturday night! Well, you're going to tell me all about it. But first, you need a bath!"

Lily stood up, walked into the closet and came back with a large, white robe.

"Don't worry, this doesn't belong to anyone. Mom buys a new one every time we take on a foster kid or someone stays with us temporarily. It's clean. And you'll find brand new towels in the bathroom, too. Go ahead and spend as much time as you need. I'll have dad bring up your things. You got a change of clothes? Or something halfway decent?" she asked.

Thomas thought a moment. He had packed more than he had used, so there should be some fresh clothes in his bag. A pair of shorts and a t-shirt were all he needed. He nodded to Lily.

"Yeah, I should have something clean in my bag with the rest of my stuff," he admitted.

"Good. Now, go shower! And you better wash behind those ears, young man...I'm gonna check!" she said, wagging her index finger at him.

With that, she walked to the door leading back to the hall, pausing for just a moment.

"By the way, there are three doors in that bathroom. This one that leads into your room, another that opens into the hallway, and a third one that leads into Bobby's old room," she instructed him.

"Who's Bobby?" Thomas inquired.

"Just my older brother. He's off at college now," Lily said, closing the door behind her.

Although Thomas wanted nothing more than to be back at his own house, the elation from the retreat far behind him, there was a part of him that was glad he had ended up where he did. He could tell there was a reason he had come to live with the Thompson's, though he had no idea what that reason might be. And, he knew there was something special about Lily, something besides his obvious attraction to her. It felt like they were destined to have met. Perhaps, he considered, this was the only way God could have made that happen. Whatever the reason, Thomas felt excited to have a chance to find out.

# CHAPTER FIVE
## A DECISION TO MAKE

After Thomas had cleaned up and got settled, Mr. Thompson drove him to the hospital. They checked in at the front desk, found the nursing station that his mom had been assigned to, and headed over for his first visit. He approached the nurse sitting at the station, introduced himself, and asked where he could find his mom. She paused for a moment, as if not sure what to say, and then turned to Mr. Thompson. Thomas didn't think he would ever forget what happened next.

The nurse asked Ben for some identification, and questioned what his relationship was to 'the patient'. Thomas didn't like how she didn't say his mom's name. Mr. Thompson explained the situation, at which point the nurse asked them to wait, pointing to a row of chairs up against a wall. Thomas asked what was going on, and why he couldn't see his mom. The nurse said she had to check, as it wasn't her decision to make.

The two men didn't have to wait long. They had barely gotten comfortable when they heard the sound of two women talking, accompanied by the clicking of heels across the floor. A moment later, a taller woman in a lab coat came around the corner, followed closely behind by the nurse they had spoken with earlier. She held a chart in the crook of her left arm as she extended her right hand out, first to Mr. Thompson, and then to Thomas.

"Thomas, I'm Dr. Walker," she began. "Can the two of you please follow me?"

Thomas didn't like the sound of that. Every time someone asked him to follow them somewhere lately, it had been to give him bad news. Unfortunately, this time was no different. They followed Dr. Walker, entering a room halfway down the hall. It was furnished like every doctor's office Thomas had ever seen, complete with a replica human skeleton hanging in one corner. The two men were ushered into chairs facing the desk, and Dr. Walker took her seat behind it.

"So, Mr. Thompson, I'm sorry, but I have to ask, how are you related to the family?" Dr. Walked inquired.

"No relation at all. I guess I'm just the Good Samaritan in this story," Ben replied.

"Well then," Dr. Walked continued. "I'm sure you can see that puts us in a dilemma. Hospital policy states we are only to discuss a patient's condition with an adult member of the immediate family. Can I ask where his father might be?"

"Last I heard," Ben admitted, "the guy is spending some time in jail, since he was what caused his wife to be here in the first place. And before you ask, I don't know about any other relatives, or the church would have called them instead of me, I imagine." He looked at Thomas. "Thomas? Do you have any other relatives in the area?"

Thomas shook his head. "What does that matter, though? Can't I just go see my mom? What's the deal?"

Dr. Walker tapped her fingers on the top of the clipboard, obviously deep in thought. Before she could say anything, Ben reached back for his wallet, pulled it out, removed a document, and unfolded it for Dr. Walker to read. She took the document, scanned it thoroughly, frowning just slightly as she did, and then handed it back to Ben.

"Would you mind if we got a copy of that before you leave?" she asked.

"Not at all. I figured you might need one. I can have your nurse take care of it now, while you talk to the boy." He began to stand up, then turned to face Thomas. "Unless you'd rather I stayed?"

Thomas wasn't sure what to say, but with the feeling he had in the pit of his stomach, he figured it would probably be best to have Mr. Thompson nearby.

"Yeah, stay. I'm not sure what's going on, but I'm feeling like I don't want to be alone right now."

Ben sat back down, placing one hand on Thomas' forearm, saying "Sure thing kid. I'm here for ya."

After a brief pause, Dr. Walker set the clipboard down, focusing her attention on Thomas.

"Thomas, your mom got here in pretty bad shape. I don't know all that happened, but she was pretty banged up. A few broken bones, a dislocated jaw. The surgery she was under was to set the breaks, fix her jaw, and generally check her over for anything we didn't see right away." Another pause. "At some point during the surgery, we noticed she wasn't doing so well. There were internal injuries that we weren't aware of. Those injuries, plus the amount of stress her body was under from the pain, well, she had a complication."

Thomas couldn't take his eyes off Dr. Walker, his face a blank expression as he listened carefully. Inside, it was taking every ounce of his energy to not scream out loud. Fighting back the fear and anger, his voice cracked as the words barely squeaked out, "Is she dead?"

"She's in a coma right now. We honestly don't know for how long. Her heart failed, twice. The second time we almost didn't get it started back up. But, we've got her on medication that should help, and she has round the clock supervision. We're giving her the best care we possibly can, you have to trust that."

Thomas felt his world fall apart. Far, far down below him, he could see the happiness he had felt just a few hours before, riding home from the retreat, his entire life plan laid out before him. Now, he felt like he was falling into an abyss, and falling fast. His eyes jumped from Dr. Walker to Mr. Thompson and back so many times, he couldn't count.

"Can...can...can I...see her?" he mumbled.

"Well, I can't let you in the room with her just now. She's in Intensive Care. But yes, I can take you to see her. I need to prepare you before we go down there, though. There's a lot of machines making all sorts of noises. And, she probably doesn't look much like you remember her the last time you saw each other. I want you to be prepared, okay?"

Thomas nodded without really understanding.

Dr. Walker picked up the clipboard again, tapped the top corner for a moment or two, and then stood up.

"Okay. Let's go," she said.

They walked back down the hallway to the Nurses Station, pausing only long enough for Mr. Thompson to let the nurse make a copy of the document he had presented earlier. After that, they called an elevator, riding it up to the Intensive Care floor. Dr. Walker asked them to wait in a small lobby while she spoke with the attending nurse on duty, then waved them to follow. Down another hallway and through two sets of doors that swung open as they approached, they finally arrived. Dr. Walker pointed to a wall that was all windows from about the knees up.

"Your mom is in room number three. You can see her from that window right there. I'm going to speak to Mr. Thompson for a moment." She paused. "Thomas, remember, she's not going to look like herself at all. And she probably won't know you're there. We'll come join you in a moment."

Thomas walked the few last steps to the window hesitantly, afraid of what he might find, and yet far more afraid of not seeing her. He had to know. Behind him, he could hear Mr. Thompson and the doctor speaking in hushed tones. He didn't even try to make out what they were saying. All his attention was on what might be waiting for him once he was close enough to see inside.

When he was close enough to see inside the room, his attention was immediately drawn to the machines. There must have been a dozen of them, stacked up against every wall, wires running everywhere. Inside the room, sitting on a small chair, a nurse was reading over charts, her back turned so she couldn't see him approach.

The woman lying in the bed looked nothing like his mom. In fact, the resemblance was so far off, he had to look at the nameplate by the door to ensure he hadn't somehow approached the wrong window. The hair was the same color, what he could see of it. And he thought the one hand he could see looked as he remembered. But nothing else he saw told him he was looking at his mom. What he could see of her face, the parts around the oxygen mask that covered her nose and mouth, was swollen and purple. Her eyes looked like tiny, wrinkled eggplants.

His emotions went into a tailspin, fluctuating between despair, anguish, frustration and anger, bordering on hate. He thought about his father, sitting in some prison cell, wishing it was him lying on that hospital bed.

He found himself silently making a promise that one day if he had anything to do with it, it would be. How could someone who had made a promise to care for and love someone else, for better or worse, do such a thing? It was far beyond Thomas' ability to comprehend. All he knew was, it wasn't right. He also felt like he should have been there. He should have protected her somehow. He knew his dad was twice his size, but still, he could have done something, would have done something, if not for that stupid retreat.

Thomas felt his knees give way as his body collapsed to the floor. Within a couple of seconds, Dr. Walker and Mr. Thompson were at his side. Dr. Walker checked his pulse, put her hand against his forehead, and then flashed a small penlight in each of his eyes. Satisfied, she nodded to Mr. Thompson and the two of them helped Thomas into a sitting position, his back to the wall. Inside, he wanted to cry, but he couldn't find the strength to do even that. Emptiness never felt so heavy.

For the rest of the visit, Thomas was in a fog. He heard Mr. Thompson ask permission to call Dr. Walker in the morning, making sure the doctor had his cell and work phone numbers in case she needed to reach him. The two adults spoke for another minute or two at a distance far enough from where Thomas sat that he couldn't make out everything they said. One part he did make out, though. As the words registered in his muddled, cloudy mind, they cut him to the core.

*"I'm giving her less than a twenty percent chance she'll wake up this week, and even less that she'll make it through the next twenty-four hours."*

On the drive home, Thomas asked Ben about the document he had given to Dr. Walker.

"Oh, that. That was a copy of the Temporary Custody order we had cut this afternoon. It basically says my wife and I have legal custody of you until your mom or dad is able to take care of you again. You see, Terri and I have been foster parents for about ten years now. Just something we do to help out those in need. We have all those extra bedrooms, and we can afford to do whatever we need to in situations like yours so teens in similar circumstances get the help they need," he told him.

"So, I'm going to stay with you guys more than just a few nights?" Thomas asked.

"Yeah, Thomas. It looks like you might be with us for a while now. Hopefully not too long, maybe a couple of weeks. But it was either that or let you stay at some half-way house until the state found you a more permanent place. And trust me, you don't want to ever stay at one of those," Ben replied.

Thomas thought about it. He liked the Thompson's, and he definitely liked the room he had been given to use. He also wouldn't mind seeing Lily more. But he didn't want to be separated from Julianna. He knew she would need him, and he knew he absolutely needed her. She was the last piece of his broken family that was still intact. He was afraid Julianna might not have the same options he had, that the people she was living with wouldn't want her to stay. If Ben didn't want him to stay at a half-way house, maybe he wouldn't want Julianna to wind up there either. He had to try.

"Mr. Thompson? I mean, Ben? Can I ask a favor?" he meekly whispered.

"Sure can," Ben replied.

"Don't let Julianna go to one of those half-way houses either, okay?" he mumbled between sobs. "She's all I got left."

Ben didn't say anything at first, just sat in silence staring out the front window of his car as they drove.

"I promise you, Thomas. I'll call Amanda tomorrow, and we'll work something out. You won't lose her. I won't let that happen," he replied softly.

Back at the house, Thomas walked numbly down the hall, ignoring an inquiry from Mrs. Thompson. He caught a brief glimpse of Lily sitting at the dinner table, a look of concern and shock on her face, a fork still halfway in her mouth. He woodenly lumbered up the stairs, down the hall, and into his temporary room. His bag from the retreat was there, next to a stack of his clothes, once more, clean and folded neatly on the bed. Next to those were four bags from Target, the result of Terri and Lili's shopping trip. Just looking at the bags gave Thomas the ominous feeling that he would be here for a long, long stay. Not even bothering to look inside, he simply pushed everything off the bed, put his headphones on, laid down, and fell asleep.

In the morning, the empty feeling was still there, as it was the next day and the next. Over time, and over many late night talks with Lily, Thomas began to sense the only way to get rid of the feeling was to confront his dad. He wanted to tell him how angry he was, how disappointed he was, and how hopeless he and his sister felt without their parents around. At one point, Lily suggested he ask her dad for advice, and Thomas agreed. Together, he and Ben worked on a letter Thomas could share with his father. Ben had informed him that trying to find the right words in the moment during a situation like this was difficult. He showed him how to formulate his emotions into sentences that shared his anger and pain, yet didn't come off accusatory or insulting. After several drafts, the two were comfortable with the letter.

On the way to the jail, Thomas imagined the conversation he would have after reading the letter to his dad. He watched as, in his mind, his father broke down crying, begged him for forgiveness and promised never to do anything like that again. He saw the sorrow and remorse his father felt for the actions he had taken, imagining his dad reaching out for a hug. Little did he realize how far from the truth his imaginary conversation would be.

At the jail, Thomas was led into a room that held nothing but a small table and two chairs. The guard who escorted him in pointed to one of the chairs and asked him to wait while someone brought his dad over. Before he left, the guard looked at Thomas curiously.

"You sure you want to do this, kid?" he inquired.

"He's my dad. I have to," he replied staunchly.

With that, the guard left the room, shutting the door behind him. During the wait, Thomas read the letter again, over and over, each time changing the emphasis on certain words. He wanted to make sure he got it right. After several read-throughs, he was distracted by a nagging pull at the edges of his senses. At first, he passed it off as nervousness. But as it grew stronger, he realized it had a certain, familiar feel.

His skin began to tingle and the hairs on his arms and neck stood straight. The air smelled like gunpowder, reminding him of the scent that lingered after a fireworks show. It hung around him, feeling heavy and warm, while a metallic taste filled the back of his throat, causing Thomas to retch. The last time he sensed this was that day he was on retreat, while Father Dominic delivered a talk. There was no doubt about it this time. The darkness had returned.

Thomas suddenly felt uneasy, realizing this time there was nowhere to run, and no one would come looking even if he did. His mind raced as he sought an escape. Finding none, he prepared himself for the inevitable. His hands closed tightly on the seat of the chair, his shoulders stiffened and rose upward. He sat as straight as he could, forcing his head to turn in the direction of the door. As if he could see through the wall, Thomas saw a shape like a dark cloud on the other side of the concrete and steel. The cloud moved slowly and deliberately towards the door. He heard the click of the lock as the door slid open.

A man entered the room, head bowed down, eyes locked on the floor. His hands were shackled in front of him and his feet were chained. He looked nothing like Thomas thought he should. All those days playing catch, helping rake the leaves, or washing the family car; Thomas had never seen his father like this. His hair was ragged and dirty, he needed a shave. The usual confidence his father carried was gone, replaced with an empty, hollow worthlessness. No, it was not the same man he had seen just a few weeks back. That man had been smiling as he waved goodbye. That man was his dad, not this one. Thomas remembered watching from the back window of the bus until his dad had been out of sight. Had he known that would be the last time he would see his dad like that, he never would have got on that bus.

Thomas looked at the guard standing behind his father, hoping for an explanation. But the guard simply unlocked the chains, reminded both men he would be standing outside the door, and then left the room. Thomas was alone with a man who carried within him the same dark and evil presence that Thomas had fled from once before. At some point in the past few weeks, he realized the man who stood before him now had ceased to be his father. The withdrawn shell of a man wearing orange overalls took a seat on the chair across the table from Thomas. He sat sideways, not facing Thomas directly, his head still fixed towards the floor.

For the first few minutes, the two simply sat there. Thomas stared with trepidation at the caricature of the man he once loved sitting before him. Gone from his mind were any thoughts about reading the letter he had with him. He doubted the man before him would even comprehend the words. Yet, he knew something had to be said. Thomas forced himself to lean forward slightly, urging his father to look him in the eyes while dreading what might happen if he did.

"Dad?" he started, weakly. "Are you okay?"

His father snorted a reply, spittle spraying from his mouth. Thomas thought he saw an evil grimace flash briefly across the man's face.

"Dad, it's Thomas, your son," the words stumbled across Thomas' lips.

When there was no reply, Thomas closed his eyes and reached down deep inside, searching in vain for a stable place to hide his fear. With his eyes closed, he could see the darkness that consumed his dad. Its presence was as real as anything else in that room. The darkness danced and sparked and electrified the air around him. With each flash, the smell of gunpowder and sulfur intensified. He imagined what he saw must be like the inside of a storm cloud, buffeted by lightning and wind. The anger he had felt for his father was suddenly replaced with a burning desire to help the man. He couldn't let his father give up like this. He had to do something. Thomas felt the sensation of being watched. Cautiously, he opened his eyes.

Thomas jumped, almost falling out of his chair. Cold, black orbs peered back at him through half-closed lids. An ominous hollow voice mouthed words stained with hate.

"I'm not your dad," the voice announced. "You should go. Leave now. Don't come back. Go find someone new to be your father. I don't want you anymore."

Thomas fought back tears. He was so tired of crying. He tried to do something else, anything else. He wanted to shout, to tell his dad to fight the darkness, but the words wouldn't form. Instead, he simply sat there, sobbing. The man stood up, walked to the door and called for the guard to take him back to his cell. As the door began to close, leaving him alone once more, Thomas heard a menacing laugh echo through his mind.

On the way home, he didn't say a word. He knew Ben asked him at least one question, maybe more. But he didn't have the strength to speak. He was too busy staring into an abyss of despair, loneliness, and fear. Try as he might to resist, Thomas fell. For days he wandered through life aimlessly with no direction and no hope. The abyss was deep, much deeper than it had been before. It almost swallowed him forever. Had it not been for the patience and caring nature of Lily, and the stubbornness of Julianna, who hugged him every time she saw him, he might not have come out alive.

The days turned into weeks, weeks stretched into months, until, here he was, five months later, still living in the same bedroom at the Thompson's. As was usually the case, it was late at night, and he was awake. Although it was a school night, he couldn't sleep. As he lay on the bed upside down, with his head near the bottom and his feet at the top, he reached out with his mind to the person lying next to him. Lily lay stretched out the opposite way. About three feet separated the two. Yet, for Thomas, space didn't matter. He had learned that the tingling sensation he felt that day in the prison didn't happen only when the darkness was around. He had begun to sense it almost daily. Though it would still come and go, he felt it was getting stronger.

What it was, exactly, he didn't know. All he knew was, when he felt it, if he closed his eyes, he saw images in his mind. The images took on different shapes and colors, and he was convinced that, at times, they were accompanied by different smells. He had noticed that the shapes tended to change depending on the moods of the people around him. One day, when the sensation was particularly strong, he saw an image floating in the air above Julianna. The shape was bright, blue and fluffy. Later that same day, after Julianna had become angry with one of the local kids in the neighborhood, her image became wispy and light gray, like smoke.

Most of the time he brushed it off, thinking it was most likely just his imagination. He never shared with anyone what it was that he saw. Not even with Lily. How could he? Her image was almost always a shade of red, from a light coral to a deep crimson. Red was the color of love, of passion. There was no way he could tell her that he saw these things inside of her. Nor could he share with her how he felt, not how he really felt. He thought she was supposed to be like his big sister. Yet, the longer he stayed at the Thompson's, he couldn't deny he felt something more. Lily was definitely his best friend.

Regardless of his mood, she had a way of bringing a little sunlight into the storm of his life. Somehow, she always knew when he was struggling, and would simply show up, knocking softly at his door from the bathroom. They spent those nights awake, Thomas lying face down across the foot of his bed, her sitting against the headboard, two pillows propped behind her. She always sat with one leg crossed under her, the other one dangling over the side. A few times, deep into the last hours of the evening, their conversation paused just long enough to let him drift into slumber. He hated those nights because they meant he would wake up to find her gone.

This night, however, they were both wide awake. He had finally reached a point where he felt comfortable and safe enough with her that he shared the story of what happened to him on the retreat. Although, when it got to the point of telling her about the lunch he had with Father Dominic, he hesitated. It wasn't that he didn't want her to know about his decision to become a priest, it was that he was no longer sure himself. He no longer knew what his future would look like. His dad was the one who brought in all of the income, and since he was in jail right now, and his mom still in a coma, Thomas had no idea what that meant for his plans. Though, like with most things he was hesitant to share, Lily knew there was more to the story.

"So, that's it. You guys just had lunch, and that was all?" she asked incredulously.

"Well, yeah…I guess," Thomas replied. "I mean, there were all those other kids around and stuff."

Lily looked at him for a moment longer, then shook her head. "Thomas. I know we haven't known each other for long, but I think I got you figured out. You have 'a tell' when you're trying to hide something," she said.

"A tell? What's that?" he asked.

"You know, like in poker? It's something your face does when you're lying. And you've got one," she informed him.

Thomas thought about it for a moment. He knew he cared a great deal for Lily. Definitely more than just a friend, that much he knew for sure. On one hand, she was the older sibling he never had, and on the other, the best friend he always wanted but hadn't been able to keep for long. And she was so good with Julianna; teaching her different ways to do her hair, helping her choose outfits, working with her on her homework. Julianna definitely needed someone like Lily to help her get through this situation, which was fine with Thomas. It wasn't that he didn't want his little sister to come to him anymore, it was just that he never felt like he had anything to offer her. He definitely didn't have any answers, and since he was hurting inside just as much as she was, he really couldn't offer her much empathy either.

More than once, when he watched Lily and Julianna together, he had found himself thinking, if he ever did wind up getting married, he would want someone like Lily to spend his life with. Maybe that was why he didn't want to tell her about his decision to be a priest. Maybe he cared for her more than he admitted to himself. Suddenly, he had to find out.

Thomas rolled on his side, facing Lily. He was nervous about what he was about to ask her, far more than he should be if they were truly just friends.

"Lily?" he asked pensively, feeling his hands start to sweat and his lower lip tremble.

"Um...yeah?" she replied cautiously, as if she could somehow sense what might be coming.

"Do you love me?"

The words came out sounding hollow, almost as empty as he felt inside. Lily smiled at first as if she thought it might be a joke. But then, seeing the seriousness in his gaze, her face lost all semblance of joviality.

"I don't know, Thomas. I mean, of course, I do. In one way, you're kinda like a brother to me," she admitted.

Thomas winced, hoping his 'poker face' didn't indicate his discomfort. He was about to turn back over and forget he had ever said anything when she continued, "But then, I don't think as much about Bobby as I do about you, so I know what I'm feeling is somehow different. I don't know if I'd call it love, though…maybe just a really, really strong like? Can we do with that for now?"

Thomas thought about it, looking away. Since he wasn't completely convinced that he felt much more than she had just admitted, he was willing to let it go for now. Suddenly, he felt her hand on his. He hadn't even heard her move. When he looked back, she was close enough to kiss. And so he did. Softly, gently. Not passionately. Just enough to know their lips had touched.

Pulling away, he kept his eyes on her face, hoping to read her reaction. At first, she just sat there, her eyes closed. Slowly, a tiny smile began to grow. Pulling gently at the corners of her mouth, the smile cautiously filled her whole face. Thomas could see that her eyes smiled too, even though they were still closed. He licked his lips, tasting her lip gloss for the first time. It tasted exactly as it smelled. Sweet, like candy, with a flavor of cherries, or maybe strawberries. He couldn't be sure, and so he licked his lips again. Definitely cherries. Lily opened her eyes, gazing at him softly. Her eyes were moist and twinkled as they held his.

"That was by far the best first kiss I think I've ever had," she said in a whisper, as if suddenly afraid someone would find them together.

Thomas didn't know what to say. He wanted to kiss her again, so he leaned in once more. Lily stopped him with a single finger against his lips. Slowly, she drew a line from his mouth to his ear, then wrapped her hand around the back of his head, pressing their foreheads together. She sighed.

"I think once was enough for tonight. I doubt either of us expected this. Let's just hold this moment, for now," she suggested.

Thomas nodded. He knew she was right. They shouldn't get involved with each other right now. For one, the Thompson's had been so kind to let him live in their house. He felt a little guilty like he would be violating their trust. And, for another, Lily was leaving soon. It was only two months until the end of school, and she would be graduating, going off to college, leaving him far behind. And, finally, what he really needed right now more than anything, was a friend. He knew having a romantic relationship could jeopardize their friendship, make things difficult around the house, and perhaps even cause problems between Lily and Julianna. There were times Thomas hated his virtuous side.

Lily gently squeezed the back of his head where her hand still held him, then sat back against the headboard once more. Thomas rolled back over onto his stomach, savoring the warm glow that permeated the room.

# CHAPTER SIX
## THE STORM BEFORE THE CALM

As the weeks went by, Thomas began to slowly lose his support network. Father Dominic left in late April for a mission trip to Panama. In early May, the Confirmation and Youth Group programs shut down for the summer. Amanda left soon after for a mission of her own; building schools in Mexico. Ben and Terri were still there, but Thomas felt more and more distant from them. He couldn't get over how often, just by their presence, they reminded him of his own parents. It was nothing they did, it was just the situation, and Thomas knew that. Still, he couldn't get past it.

For the most part, he remained polite in his conversations with Terri. He just couldn't be open and honest with her. Anytime he started to, he was reminded how much he would rather be sharing his thoughts with his mom, and he would shut down, resort to one-word answers, grunts, or shoulder shrugs. But with Ben, it was different. The anger Thomas carried for his dad was simply too heavy. Some of it spilled over on Ben, even though he did nothing to provoke or deserve it. At times, Thomas found himself being downright rude to the man.

His relationship with Julianna changed too. Perhaps she was also reminded of the family she lost whenever he was around. Thomas didn't know for sure but honestly didn't feel like asking. He was dealing with his own problems, which were more than enough. There were days when she had come to him, and he had simply pushed her away. Inside, he still loved his sister, and he really did want to be there for her, but there just wasn't enough of him left inside to share. And so he ignored her requests to talk, stopped letting her come to him for comfort and support. No longer did they share headphones, her arm wrapped around his chest, falling asleep in the comfort of knowing they still had each other.

Instead, she had been told in no uncertain terms that she was now required to ask permission to enter his room. He had told her it was because he was getting older, that he needed his privacy. In reality, he knew if Lily poked her head in the door and saw that Julianna was already in there, she would tell him she would come back later. Simply put, he had chosen Lily over Julianna. And though he had never said it out loud, she definitely felt it. And so, he pushed her away, and she left in tears, until one day she stopped trying. What Julianna didn't know, though, was that on those days, Thomas cried too. He missed the big brother he used to be. He knew that person was still inside him, lost down deep in the chasm that plagued his soul, covered by the emotions and frustrations of all he had endured. He just wasn't strong enough to pull the old Thomas out of that pit. He wasn't sure anyone was.

In truth, all he had left was Lily. But she, too, eventually left. The day after graduation, Lily boarded a plane bound for a two-month tour of Europe. They kept in touch via text, but it wasn't the same. He couldn't find the words, or the courage, to tell her what was really going on inside, how it felt like he was slowly fading away. All he had to prove he was still real, was his anger at his dad and his despair for his mom. Nothing positive found its way through the cracks between the anger and despair. To protect himself from breaking apart, Thomas had effectively shut out the world. If only he had realized, in his struggle for strength, how vulnerable he had become.

In some ways, he had to try and protect himself. The strange feelings and weird shapes were getting stronger and becoming more frequent. When he saw Julianna in tears, he didn't just feel bad for her, it was like he could feel her sorrow. When he was near Ben or Terri, he didn't just see how happy they were, he could feel it too. He had even experienced this sensation a few times with people he didn't know.

One Sunday, as he was sitting in church, he had become overwhelmed with the emotions of the people around him. People desperate for answers, people hungry to find God, some at the edge of despair. The onrush forced him to walk out. He lied to Ben after church was over, said he had felt nauseous and dizzy. In truth, he had, though not from being sick. Instead, the nausea had come from his inability to digest that many emotions at once. Still, he didn't tell anyone about it. He was afraid they would think he was some kind of freak. To be honest, he was beginning to wonder that about himself.

And so, day after day, he dragged his way through his life, spending more and more time on his own. The few friends he had from school all lived on the other side of town, where his old house was. Slowly, piece by piece, he had lost everything he had known, everything he had been comfortable with. He was in pain, but he couldn't find the strength to shout out loud, only silently, inside his own mind.

To make things worse, the feelings he had for Lily hadn't gone away, even though he knew it wouldn't work out between them. Not only was she two years older, but as soon as she got back from Europe, she would be five hundred miles away at college. The only thing that brought his spirits up was getting her text messages. Every time his phone buzzed, his heart jumped, hoping it would be her. This last time it buzzed, he reached for the phone with anticipation. His emotions climbed even further when he saw the message was from Lily. Filled with hope, he opened the text and then froze.

His moment of expectant joy turned to jealous fear as he looked at the image on his phone. The picture was of a group of people, including Lily, three of her friends, and a handful of guys Thomas had never seen. The group stood in pairs, arms around each other's necks, smiling broadly. The message she had written under the picture said, *"Look at how tan I'm getting! I'm as dark as the locals!"* Looking at her was the last thing he wanted to do. At least not as long as she had some strange guy from another country with his arm around her. Especially because he knew there was nothing he could do about it.

Two things happened almost at once. The first was that an overwhelming sensation of emotions from those nearby flooded in. He felt the happiness Julianna and Terri shared as they joked and laughed with each other. He felt tension, anger, and frustration coming from Ben as he argued with someone on a business call. He could even feel the quiet sense of boredom coming from the gardener as he trimmed a rose bush out back. And second, he sensed the darkness once more. The familiar smell, the metallic taste, the tingling in the air. Thomas was already far too familiar with the demons calling card.

Thomas felt like he was drowning. He had to get out of the house. He knew if he stayed inside, something bad was going to happen. His anger was quickly building into a furious rage. He was furious with Lily for leaving him and furious at his dad for giving up. He was even angry with his mom for not waking up from her coma. He was angry at Julianna for needing too much from him and angry at himself for knowing he couldn't give her what she needed. He was angry at Ben and Terri for trying to be so nice to him all the time. And he was definitely mad at God. As far as he was concerned, God had just lost himself a priest.

Heading out to the garage, he grabbed one of Bobby's old bicycles. He didn't worry about where he would go, as long as it wasn't here. Pedaling as fast as he could, Thomas rode away, hoping to clear the jumble of emotions assailing his mind. Although it was still morning, it was already unseasonably warm. The heat outside his body challenged the heat he felt inside, causing him to pedal so hard, his control started to slip. He skidded wildly around corners. Every person he passed added to the emotions brewing in his heart.

At one turn, he almost hit a young woman pushing a stroller. From the baby, he picked up the feelings of excitement and awe. From the woman, despair, and hopelessness. He somehow knew her husband had recently left her, and that she was desperate to know how she would survive with two kids and a new baby. Thomas could tell that she was on the verge of giving up. Her despair frightened him. It was even darker than his own.

On another part of the path, he scared an older couple who hadn't heard him approach until he was right on top of them. The man was worried about his wife. Thomas somehow understood that her health wasn't what it used to be, and the old man was afraid he was losing her. The woman, however, just seemed lost, confused, as if her world, including even her husband beside her, was no longer familiar at all. He yelled for them to get out of the way, causing the old man to stumble into his wife, both of them falling to the ground. Thomas ignored the new emotions of panic and anger he felt from the man. He was on a mission. Somewhere out there was a release for all of this. Somewhere he would find what he needed, even if he rode for the rest of his life.

Thomas reached the shopping center in record time, breathing hard and deep, his shirt soaked in sweat. The back of his mouth tasted sour from the mixture of rapidly breathing warm air blending with the acid of his emotions. He tried to spit but couldn't, his mouth was far too dry. Parking his bike against the side of the first building he came to, he went inside to get a drink. Five minutes later, a little cooler and breathing a bit slower, he came back out, only to find his bike was gone. Looking around to see if perhaps he had parked it somewhere else, he caught a glimpse of five kids, all about his age, running through the parking lot. The biggest one was riding his bike. This was the outlet his anger had been searching for.

Thomas rushed after the thieves, his boiling anger feeding his muscles with enough energy to run faster than he had ever run before. As he did, he felt the darkness close in, surrounding him, his body absorbing it with every step. Thomas didn't care anymore. He gave in to the darkness, and as he did, he felt a powerful strength surge within. Before the boys knew he was coming, he had caught up to the group, taking the first kid by complete surprise. Thomas launched himself into the boy's waist, tackling him from behind, causing them both to spill to the pavement. The boy's face hit the ground with a crack. The sound caught the attention of another of the kids, who shouted a warning to his friends. The four still standing raced away, their theft of the bike more important than helping their downed friend.

Thomas scrambled back up, a wicked sneer darkening his face. He paused just long enough to look at the kid he had just tackled. There would be no return assault from this one. The boy was far more concerned with the blood oozing from the gash on his forehead than retaliation.

"One down...four to go," Thomas said as he turned towards the other four.

Opening more fully to the power he felt as the darkness filled his body and mind, Thomas rushed forward again, grabbing a fist-sized rock as he ran. He threw it as hard as he could, somehow knowing it would hit true. He watched the rock sail through the air, arc downward, and strike the shoulder of the boy riding the bike. The boy twisted suddenly, turning the front wheel drastically to the side, bike and rider cartwheeling over each other. The boy got up, blood coming from one elbow, both knees, and his left palm.

"Oh, you're gonna pay for that," the boy said.

"Give me back my bike," Thomas demanded as he skidded to a stop, his eyes burning with anger and his fists clenched tight.

"You left it. We found it. That makes it ours. But, if you really want it, come get it!" the larger boy challenged, walking with determination towards Thomas, and tossing the bike to the side.

Two of the other boys circled around behind him, putting Thomas in the middle of the four. The largest one, the kid who had been riding the bike, closed the gap, taunting Thomas. Behind him and just to one side, the fourth kid was following behind. Thomas looked around for some kind of weapon, anything he could get his hands on. Seeing nothing, his instincts took over. With burning rage, Thomas rushed at the biggest kid, his arms stretched wide as if he was about to tackle him. Startled, the boy stopped his advance and instead prepared to attack. He raised his arm back behind his head, ready to punch Thomas the first chance he could.

Thomas saw all of this as if in slow motion. The moment his assailant made the decision to prepare to punch him, he knew it before the boy's arm had even moved. As if looking into the future, he could see the point where the punch would land even before the fist traveled towards him. Moving with amazing speed and grace, Thomas ducked, spinning under the swinging arm. Rather than tackle the boy as his actions had appeared he would, the spin put him directly in front of another member of the gang. A well-placed punch from Thomas dropped the kid out cold. His limp body slumped to the ground in a tumbled heap.

"Two down," Thomas growled, turning to face the remaining three.

Thomas could feel the emotions of the final three boys begin to change. The confidence and bravado they had earlier displayed were rapidly fading away. Thomas knew he had gained the upper hand. Breathing deeply, the smell of sulfur thick and heavy in the air, he reached inside his heart, gathering every negative emotion he had. His anger at his dad, frustration with not being able to talk to his mom, the jealousy he felt for that kid in the photo with Lily, his embarrassment at not being the brother he needed to be for Julianna all mixed together. Thomas let the emotions swirl and blend feeling his power growing stronger still. He knew he was going to hurt these kids. He was going to do to them what he wished he could have done to his father.

The three remaining boys stood frozen, unsure what to do. Taking the initiative, Thomas rushed head-long towards the closest one. As the boy steadied himself for the attack, Thomas launched feet first, his heels driving into the boy's knee, his legs bending awkwardly. The stress was too much for the leg, and a sickening crunch sounded as it broke a few inches above the ankle. Thomas turned to face the final two, his face no longer recognizable as it twisted into a grimace of hate.

"Who's next?" Thomas growled menacingly.

The smaller of the two looked the most frightened, and Thomas turned his attention to him, walking towards him with a dark, determined stride. He didn't even care that this placed the largest kid at his back where he couldn't see him. His instincts told him it wouldn't take much to deal with the smaller one in front. Then he'd be left with only one.

"Look, man, you can have the bike back, okay? We didn't know it belonged to anyone. We thought it was abandoned," the smaller boy pleaded with him.

"Bullshit! I wasn't in that restaurant for long. You had to see me ride into the parking lot. You took it from me, and you know it," Thomas replied.

As he was about to grab the boy he faced, Thomas felt a tingling at his right side. Without even looking, he ducked, spinning to his left, watching a fist sail through the space where his head had been just a moment ago. Still spinning, Thomas brought his right knee up, landing heavily against the larger boys' stomach. The boy grunted as the impact spun him around. With the wind knocked out of him, he fell. Without hesitation, Thomas jumped on top, his fists raining down on the boy's face, shoulders and chest. The boy cried out for him to stop, but Thomas couldn't stop. The darkness had him now. He was buried somewhere inside his own mind, watching the scene play out as if he wasn't really there. With each punch, he could hear the darkness laughing, mocking him for being weak, driving its tendrils of hate and fear deeper into Thomas' heart.

Thomas stood back up, the darkness now fully in control. The kid he had just beat moaned painfully as he curled into a fetal position. Blood oozed from a split lip and both nostrils. The last of the boys still standing took one look at Thomas, his eyes wide with fear, and then turned and ran back towards the restaurant where they had found the bike. Thomas was fast on his heels. As they reached the sidewalk in front of the restaurant, Thomas caught him from behind and spun the kid around, fist raised high in the air to strike. As he was about to pound his fist into the terrified face, he caught a glimpse of his reflection in the restaurant window. At first, he didn't even recognize himself. There was blood on his shirt, his pants were ripped across his left knee, and he was covered in dirt and sweat. His hair was windblown and crazy, giving his face a strange, distant look. But what Thomas noticed most, was his eyes.

Those eyes! They couldn't be his! They looked nothing like the pair he saw in the mirror. They just couldn't be his. It was then he realized he was no longer looking at himself. What he saw instead filled him with remorse and fear. He saw hatred, anger, violence.

He saw the Devil.

He saw his dad.

This was the face his dad had all those nights when his parents had fought. Those eyes had scared him back then, even though he never admitted it. And now, those eyes were inside his own head looking back out. Thomas knew he had one hope left, only one thing that would free him from the darkness that held him.

His mind searched frantically for the strength to put his thoughts into words. He could feel the darkness moving to stop him. It was aware of what he was trying to do, and Thomas could feel it try to resist. There wasn't much time. He had to strike now, or he would wind up a hollow, empty shell like his father. With every ounce of strength he could muster, Thomas spoke.

*"Jesus, I surrender."*

Lightning flashed inside his mind, crashing through the darkness with a deafening roar. Thomas stumbled. Had he not still been holding the other boy's shirt, he would have fallen down. The light penetrated deep into his heart, burning brighter with each heartbeat, dissolving every last shadow of the darkness, returning him to the light. Thomas was free.

He let go of the kid's shirt, listening to the sounds of the boy's feet pounding the pavement as he ran away. Thomas didn't care. He couldn't stop staring at his reflection in the window, hating himself for what he had become. He might be free from the darkness, but he knew he should never have let it in, should never have given it an open door to his heart. He was stronger than that.

In the reflection of the window, he saw the four boys he had fought with still lying on the ground behind him. Thomas had never hurt anyone like that before. The memories of what he had just done brought uncontrollable nausea deep from within. His knees wobbled as he bent at the waist, vomiting out the putrid sensations he felt as he realized what he had done. Unable to take it any longer, Thomas grabbed a metal chair from one of the outdoor tables. With every last bit of energy he had, he hurled it at the front window, shattering it with a crash.

Emotionally and physically spent, he collapsed to the ground, as the pain from his emotional wounds bled out through the tears in his eyes. Time passed unnoticed as he lay there screaming out his rage. Thomas wasn't aware a crowd had gathered. He didn't realize someone had called the police. He was lost in the storm.

The paramedics were the first to arrive. Two EMTs jumped out of the back door of the ambulance, followed shortly by the driver. One by one they checked over the four kids Thomas had fought with, giving the most attention to the one he had knocked unconscious. Thomas watched them through blank and empty eyes. As police cars began pulling into the lot, one of the EMTs approached Thomas to check his wounds. She wiped away the blood on his hands, checked the areas under his clothes that were stained with blood, checking to see if any of it was his. She then looked him in the eyes.

"You do all this yourself?" she asked.

Thomas said nothing.

"Well, whatever happened here, I hope they had it coming," she sighed.

"They took my bike," Thomas whispered harshly, a hollow drone in his voice. "They took my bike."

"That's a hell of a lot of damage for one bike. By the looks of it, you probably won't want it back." She nodded in the direction of the bicycle.

Thomas looked where she indicated, seeing the bike lying damaged on the ground. The front wheel was bent severely, a couple of the spokes had broken off, and the seat was torn. He shrugged.

"They took my bike," he said again, his eyes distant once more.

Two hours later, Thomas was in the back seat of Ben Thompson's car as they made their way home from the police station. Neither of them said anything for the first few miles. Finally, Thomas broke the silence.

"I'm sorry, Mr. Thompson. About the bike."

Ben sat in silence. Thomas was used to the way Ben handled problems, thinking for long periods before speaking, especially when he was obviously angry. Thomas wished his father had learned this trick. Maybe he wouldn't be in his situation if his dad had paused long enough to think before reacting so fast. Though Thomas appreciated how Ben never let his emotions take over, it made whatever he did say that much harder to hear.

Ben rarely left an open door for discussion during their talks. He was firm, yes, but always fair. He didn't say more than he had to, but never less than required. Thomas found the waiting was the toughest part. He also knew if he said anything more right now, Ben would just wait that much longer. So he simply sat there, wondering what possible punishment was pending, his mind feeding him images of what might be. None of which, he knew, would be what would eventually come to pass. Finally, Ben spoke.

"Look, Thomas, I know you've had it rough. You're stuck in some stranger's house with neither of your parents around. But right now, I guess I'm the closest thing you've got to an adult in your life, so I'm gonna tell it like it is, okay?" the lecture began.

"First thing is, you screwed up. Big time. We could have replaced the bike, filed a report, let the cops figure it out. But I think you know that, so I'm not going to belabor that point."

Ben took the first of what Thomas knew would be many small pauses.

"The good news is, you had witnesses. Even if the other kids' parents want to sue for damages, which they probably will, once the judge understands your story and hears from the witnesses who will testify that the other kids started the whole thing, he will probably throw the case out. Their kids tried to steal Bobby's bike, and you got it back. It was five against one, so it won't be easy to try and spin it like you just started fighting."

Another pause, this one long enough to make Thomas worry. Ben had never paused this long in the middle of a lecture before.

"But the window. That part I don't get. I've been scratching my head trying to understand. After the fight, when the kids were all lying on the ground or had run off, I don't get why you had to smash the window. What possibly could have motivated you to do that?"

These words hurt Thomas worse than anything had so far that day. How could he tell Ben what he saw when he had looked into that window? How could he confide in this man who had taken him in when he needed someone most? How could he admit that what had sent him over the edge in the first place was the fact that he couldn't stand being away from Lily?

Thomas began to think of all the lies he could tell Ben, stories about why he smashed the window, about what had driven him to such anger, but the next words he heard flushed those thoughts away.

"Look, I know how you feel about Lily," Ben suddenly shared.

Thomas felt his heart drop to the floor.

"It's okay. I'm not going to get angry or anything. Truth is, Terri and I have been watching the two of you. We know you guys spend a lot of time together, sometimes alone, late at night. It's a risk we take every time we foster someone. So far, Lily's played it smart. She never got close to any of the other kids we took in before."

"You two, though. Your relationship is different. I don't know if your story really touched her heart, or if she just thought you were better looking than most of the other boys we've had. Heck, maybe she just liked your personality more. You've definitely been the most sensitive teen we've fostered, and I don't mean that in a bad way. You just have a way about you of making people feel listened to and cared for. Whatever it was, something sent the two of you down that path. Terri and I could see you falling for each other.

"Luckily, we've always had a good relationship with our daughter. She came to us before we went to her. She told us about her feelings for you, promised she wouldn't let anything happen or let things get out of control. We thought about talking to the two of you together. We thought about restricting you from being around each other at night. But, after all that, I guess we just decided we'd have to trust you both.

"Heck, you'll figure this out when you're a dad. There are just so many ways you can be involved in your kids' lives. Eventually, you have to trust that you've done your job, that the lessons you taught stuck deep enough they don't make the mistakes you're afraid they might. Even though sometimes they will. But that's how we learn and grow. So you just help them put the pieces back together, and hold them when they cry."

Ben took another pause, though much smaller this time. Thomas felt his body tense.

"Well, it doesn't matter anymore. She's off in Europe, and then college. I'll just have to continue to trust the two of you will do what's right when she comes home for weekend visits and such."

This last part was said with such finality that Thomas had no choice but to accept. This was the way Ben was, how he talked. He shared only enough to let Thomas know what he was thinking, then expressed his decision, without actually saying it was a decision. He never said anything to indicate he had put his foot down, but Thomas could hear the 'thump' just the same.

"By the way, you have a visitor tonight. He arrived just before I came out to pick you up. Someone who's very concerned with what's going on in your life right now."

Thomas looked at Ben with wide eyes. He couldn't mean his father, could he?

# Chapter Seven
## Sacrifice

Thomas saw the familiar blue Honda parked in front of the house as they pulled into the garage and knew right away who had come to see him. He got out of the car, thanking Ben once more for bailing him out. Ben nodded curtly, then turned and walked towards the front door. Thomas waited until Ben was inside and then headed to the side entrance. Even though he had lived in this house now for almost eight months, he was still not comfortable using the front door. The front door was for family and invited guests. He still felt like a stray puppy, rescued from the streets, or picked up at some shelter. If the Thompson's owned a dog, they would have trained it to use the side door, and so that's the one he used.

He walked down the long hallway, reflecting back as he did every time he came in the house to the first time he had come in, wearing one of Lily's old sweaters and that hideous pair of monkey slippers. And, like every other time he thought of it, he smiled. That is until his thoughts turned to Lily, and his smile faded away. He missed her desperately. As he reached the end of the hall, the point where he had first seen Lily that day, Thomas heard the sound of a familiar voice.

"Well, well, well. You're looking a little worse for wear. Just where have you been spending your time?"

Thomas turned to glance into Ben's office, catching sight of Father Dominic seated by a small table in one corner, a coffee mug in one hand, and an open Bible in his other. It had been well over a month since the last time they had talked. Thomas noticed the man's skin was a few shades darker than it had been before. He couldn't help but grin.

"Hello, Father. How was Panama? Looks like you spent all your days on the beach," Thomas teased.

Father Dominic chuckled. "Don't I wish! Swinging hammers, digging trenches, building schools. Those are the kind of vacations I take."

"I thought you were going to be gone for a few more months," Thomas mentioned.

"I was supposed to be, yes. Had to come home for a funeral. Only here for the next week, maybe two," Father Dominic replied.

Thomas sat down in the only other chair by the table. He noticed Ben quietly close the office door, leaving the two alone. Thomas knew Father Dominic would want him to talk first, that he would simply sit there until Thomas opened the conversation.

"You probably think we should pray first, right?" Thomas inquired.

"Always a good idea. Regardless of the situation. Any ideas on which prayer we should use?" came the reply.

Thomas thought about it. Since the retreat, when Father Dominic had taught him a few, simple, easy to remember prayers, he really hadn't spent much time praying. Other than the afternoon in Amanda's office, and a couple of times when visiting with his mom, his faith life had slowed back to a crawl. Father Dominic had told him to expect it, that most teens went through similar changes after a retreat. He had told Thomas he wished there was a way to bottle up the magic that happened on retreats.

"I really haven't spent much time in prayer lately, Father. So I don't know if I'll remember any. Can you just take this one?" Thomas suggested.

Father Dominic smiled, then reached inside his robe to retrieve two mini rosaries. He handed one to Thomas.

"Then, I think it's best we ask our Blessed Mother to come join us for this talk. One decade, or two?"

Thomas groaned inside at the loaded question. There was no way he could ever say 'just one' at this point. He silently mouthed the word 'two', grinning back at Father Dominic.

"Then let's dedicate this one to Our Lady of Mount Carmel. I'll explain why later."

Father Thomas took a deep breath, letting it slowly slide back out. The two then sat for a moment in silence, the mood in the office becoming hushed and peaceful. Father Dominic started off with a prayer, asking for protection for Thomas, his family, and especially for healing for Thomas' mom, then led them twice around the mini-rosary. After they completed, Thomas handed the rosary he had used back to Father Dominic, and again they sat in silence. Thomas never knew quite what to say to begin the conversations. He was never comfortable in this moment, regardless how familiar Father Dominic was becoming to him. He glanced up at the ceiling, hoping to find the answer to his dilemma secretly written there. Finding nothing but sheetrock and paint, he opened his mouth just slightly in preparation to speak. The words came out slowly.

"So…you already know I've been in a bit of trouble…otherwise, I'm sure you would have been much more concerned about my appearance," Thomas stated, pausing to collect his thoughts. "I honestly don't know what happened. Well, that's not true. I do, and I don't, I guess. You see, it all started 'cause…well…I miss Lily. She's been like my only friend since all this happened…well, outside of you and Amanda…but you know what I mean…someone my age."

He looked up at Father Dominic, wondering how much of this story he needed to share, and what he could still keep private. And, like he did every other time he spoke with Father Dominic, whether in person or via phone, he instinctively knew that honesty was the best choice. Father Dominic had a way of sensing, already knowing, or somehow figuring out the truth anyway. So why not save time?

"I guess she's more than a friend. At least in here," Thomas tapped himself on the chest. "And with her being gone, well, now I don't really have anyone to talk to, at least not someone that really understands…you know?"

Once more Thomas paused to gather his thoughts. As easy as it was talking to Father Dominic, it was still a hard thing to openly share his feelings.

"Well…she sent me this picture…of her on the beach in Italy. She was with her friends and some other guys, I don't know who. It made me mad. Then those kids tried to steal my bike…which isn't even my bike. It's a bike I had to borrow because my bike, my real bike, is in the garage at my house…my real house," Thomas paused, looking away. "I guess I just kinda lost it."

A stillness hung in the room, as thick as canvas. Finally, Father Dominic broke the silence.

"From what I hear, you did quite a number on those boys. You're lucky it wasn't the other way around," Father Dominic said.

"Honestly, Father, they weren't all that tough. I mean, they talked a good game, like they were all gangster and stuff, but I'll bet none of them had been in a fight like that before. And…when I think about it…I'm not sure it was me doing the fighting."

Father Dominic raised one eyebrow at this, his curiosity piqued.

"Oh, really? Who was it?" he asked.

Thomas shook his head, shrugging his shoulders and scrunching his face slightly.

"No idea. But it was like I was watching from outside my body; like I wasn't in control or something. Not like I was possessed, but like I knew walking away was the right thing to do, but I couldn't. The closest I can compare it to would be like when the Hulk gets mad," Thomas admitted.

"Not uncommon for a young man your age to have raging emotions. But knowing that doesn't make it okay now, does it?" Father Dominic inquired.

Thomas nodded affirmatively. He knew his hormones were the reason a lot of his emotional episodes happened. Still, Father Dominic was right.

"When it was over, Father, and I was just standing there, looking at myself in that window…it was scary. I swear it wasn't me standing there, but some kind of demon or something. It reminded me too much of my dad and how he was with mom."

"Ah…." Father Dominic voiced. "And he's the last person in the world you want to be right now, yes?"

Thomas nodded. "Exactly…I mean…I try to remember that inside he's a good guy. Like, who knows…maybe that was how he was raised by his dad or something. Maybe yelling and throwing stuff is just what he's used to. But I don't want to end up like him. I don't want to be anything like that when I'm a dad," Thomas shared, his eyes starting to water.

"We don't get to choose the road we're on, Thomas, not even the parents we are born to. It would be nice if we could, but that's not the way life works. And just because we are part of them, and they are part of us, that doesn't mean we have to become who they are. You're absolutely right, your father's actions were most likely a product of the childhood he had. That doesn't make what he did okay, but it might help us understand.

"Come, Thomas. Let's take this conversation outside. The last time I was here, the stream behind the Thompson's house was flowing pretty strong. I hope it still is. There's something I need you to understand, and it might be better with a visual to tie it to."

Without waiting, Father Dominic stood up, heading down the hallway towards the back of the house. As they got near the patio doors leading to the backyard, Father Dominic called out, "Ben! Terri! I'm taking our little ruffian down to the creek. We'll be back for dinner!"

Terri's voice called back from somewhere in the house. "We'll be waiting, Father. Just don't get lost!"

As the two exited the house, Father Dominic whispered to Thomas, "I've been here a hundred times probably. I doubt I'd get lost! But then, one never knows what God has in store, yes?"

Thomas snorted a reply.

The pair walked to the far end of the swimming pool, and then took a small path that led around the back of a small hill that rose above the Thompson's yard. Father Dominic looked back, perhaps to make sure they were far enough away to continue the conversation.

"Thomas, I think you know the situation you are in, tough as it is, is here for a reason. There is something you are meant to learn, or understand, or discover; about yourself, about life, or maybe about your purpose for being here. It's all connected in some way. The choice regarding your circumstances might not be yours to make, but the decisions you make on how to respond is definitely in your control. In fact, that's probably the only thing you have that is truly yours. That, and your faith.

"And faith tells us, in these situations, there are always sacrifices that need to be made if we are ever going to put back the pieces that life broke apart. The way you feel about Lily is one of those sacrifices. If you really do care for her as strongly as you say you do, then you would want her to have the best life possible, wouldn't you?"

Thomas barely nodded a reply.

"Of course, you would. And I'll bet you would make a thousand different sacrifices to have your mom healed, right?"

He nodded again, this time with more conviction.

"You'd probably even be willing to sacrifice for your sister if you knew she needed it."

"Yeah, of course, I would!" Thomas blurted out.

"Then, what you have to ask yourself is, what sacrifice do you need to make to find love for your dad?"

Thomas was taken back. Love his dad? After everything he had done?

"I just don't think that's possible, Father. I'm not sure I have that within me. Plus, I don't think that's my sacrifice to make," Thomas said.

"Of course it is! The sacrifice is always ours to make. You remember the story of the Passion, the events that took place starting late on Thursday night, the days leading up to Easter, yes? We hear it every Good Friday at church." Father Dominic prompted.

"Yeah…sure. I remember," Thomas responded.

Every year, on the Friday before Easter, Thomas' church would listen to a Bible reading of the Passion of Jesus Christ. The story documents the final hours of his life, during which Jesus was betrayed by one of his closest friends, and faced the immeasurable cruelty of those who hated him until he gave up his life on the cross. He allowed himself to be tortured and killed, knowing all the while that in doing so he would save humanity.

"Well, then you'll remember the night before. Jesus had just finished the Last Supper, told Judas to go and do whatever he needed to do. He knew what was coming. In the garden that night, as he was praying, he knew what he was going to go through, and he still chose to sacrifice his own needs, his own desires. He saw the greater purpose in living for God's plan. Even after all they put him through, as he hung there on the cross, looking down at the soldiers who had beat him, mocked him, tortured him, what did he do?"

"He forgave them," Thomas recalled.

"Yes, Thomas. He sacrificed. He gave up his anger, his hatred, his human desire for revenge, and he took the cross. He owned that cross, made it his and no one else's. He forgave everyone who had put him there because he knew without them doing what they did, he would not be able to do what he was born to do."

Father Dominic paused as they reached a split in the path.

"Now, if I recall correctly, the creek we are in search of is down…this way," he said as he pointed to the path leading left.

The two continued on, the late afternoon sun disappearing as they entered into a wooded area. As they walked, Thomas thought about what Father Dominic had said about sacrifice. Try as he might, he could not find any purpose behind any of the events that had led him to now. Deep down, he knew Father Dominic was probably right, he just couldn't see how.

"I don't know, Father. Maybe I'm not strong enough. Maybe I'm not able to recognize God's plan in all of this. Maybe I don't have the ability to forgive. Maybe I don't have the faith to be a priest after all. I mean, just look at my life. I can't see how I'm on the right path."

Thomas sounded defeated, empty. Father Dominic put his hand on Thomas' forearm.

"Let me tell you something, my young man. Faith isn't judged by what you've done up to now. It's judged by the realization of the potential you find inside you. It is measured more by what you do from this moment to the next, rather than what you did until now. Look at the examples in the Bible. Saul, who we now call Paul, the greatest evangelist the church has ever had, was once its greatest persecutor. No one would have called him a man of faith before Jesus changed his name. Or St. Augustine, one of our greatest saints! He was also a man no one would call righteous before God touched his heart. Though he was born of a very devout mother, who happens to be a saint as well, Augustine's path wandered aimlessly through many temptations, most of which he fell into before finally realizing his faith. But what a faith it was once revealed!

"That's why Satan comes after those of strong faith, especially when they haven't found it yet. The more good people he can win over before they realize who they were born to be, the fewer believers he has to contend with later on. If he is hitting you this hard now, there's a reason behind it. But this is your cross to carry, your challenge to overcome. You can pray all you want for God to 'let this cup pass', but in the end, it's not up to you. Your only choice is to decide what you are going to do with the cards you've been dealt.

"Besides, there really is no 'easy' path in life. Life becomes easy only after we have taken on the greatest challenges, faced our deepest fears, risen above every trial, and witnessed our worst defeats. Then life becomes 'easy'. Nothing really changes, we just realize how strong we truly are. And what I see next to me is not someone who backs down from a fight. Heck, you took on five kids all your size and bigger! Do you really think you don't have what it takes to stand up to Satan? You have an entire host of saints and angels standing behind you. You're never alone in this fight. Never!"

Father Dominic thumped his fist into the palm of his other hand, his eyes burning with passion. Thomas had never seen him like this before.

"So, what are you saying?" Thomas asked. "That I'm just supposed to keep going? How do I know if I'm doing what's right? How do I know if I'm heading in the right direction? God doesn't leave any signs on this road we're supposed to walk. It would sure be nice if he did, but he hasn't shown me one sign. So, what, I'm just supposed to wander around out there and hope that I get it right? And then, what, wait until I die to see if I solved the puzzle?" Thomas was almost shouting now.

Father Dominic leaned back, releasing the hold he had on Thomas' arm. He still had that passionate look in his eyes, but he also knew when to give Thomas a moment to calm down. He listened to Thomas breathe, watched the tension in his jaw. When he could tell Thomas had regained some of his composure, he turned and began walking again, trusting that Thomas would follow. When he heard footsteps coming from behind, he continued on speaking.

"Yes, Thomas. That's exactly what I mean. But not with your eyes shut like they are now. This is what Jesus meant when he said, 'But blessed are your eyes, for they see, and your ears, for they hear'. This is where the Holy Spirit comes into play. It is not possible for you to know now, or ever, what the future will hold for you. Which means, yes, life will feel like everything is falling apart, but in reality, God is just putting together something new that you do not yet understand. It is not your responsibility to make every decision today, but only to be open to hearing God's word. You only need to choose what you believe is most likely the next right choice.

"Will you stumble? Of course, he expects that as well. But in each moment you will find the answer within your heart. You'll never find all the answers to life, but you can find the answer to now. By making what you believe to be the most correct choice in each moment, you'll find that in the next moment it will become that much easier to do it again.

"You see, faith is a cyclical process, a vortex if you will, expanding ever tighter with each choice you make. Each choice sends you further around the cycle to the next decision. Within this vortex, there are three driving principles. The first is Knowledge of God. When you come to know God, as you read scripture, or in prayer, or in special ways like you did on the retreat last year, this knowledge will lead you to want to take action. You'll sense a burning passion for helping others, to perform acts of true charity. These acts of charity plant more seeds of faith within you, the fruits of which are a greater love for Christ, a passion for worship.

"As this passion for worship increases, our desire to know God also grows. This leads us to further study, new ideas for charitable action, and, once more, a greater desire burns inside. But it has to start small. Your faith may be great in potential, but if you hold a seed in your hand, no wishing or dreaming or desire or skillful negotiation will ever cause that seed to grow. It must be planted, it must be tended and cared for…does this make sense, Thomas?"

Thomas nodded slowly.

"You already told me you knew in your heart what the most right choice to make was in that moment before you fought to get back your bike. You knew it would have been better to walk away, ask for help from someone else, or get the owner of that restaurant to call the cops – anything but what you did, right? Making that choice, the one that didn't end up with you sitting in a holding cell, was by far the harder choice to make. You would have to swallow your anger, swallow your pride, and ignore your emotions. But in the end, how would the outcomes have been different?"

Thomas thought about it before responding. "I guess, it's kinda like when Jesus says 'if someone takes your shirt, give them your coat too'. Like, yeah, what they did was wrong, but it doesn't help to do another wrong on top of that."

"Exactly, Thomas. But how do we do that? How do we find the space in our heart to turn off the negative emotions? How do we let love win?"

"I don't know, Father," Thomas admitted, "but something tells me I'm about to find out."

Father Dominic smiled broadly at him. "Am I that easy to predict?" he inquired jokingly.

Thomas only gave him a half-smile back, with a whimsical look on his face.

"Okay, okay...so maybe I am a little," Father Dominic admitted.

The sound of rushing water had been growing in volume as the two walked along. Now, as they came to the top of a crest, they could see the stream below.

"Here we are. Let's talk about how life flows."

# CHAPTER EIGHT
## LEARNING TO FLOW

Father Dominic took a seat on a large rock above the creek. He motioned for Thomas to take a seat on a smaller rock nearby. Thomas sat down, and then turned and looked down at the creek. It was still swollen from the spring rains, looking more like a small river than a creek. When both men had settled into a comfortable position, Father Dominic began.

"Look at the water, Thomas. What do you see?"

Thomas looked for a long time, watching the water bubbling over the rocks, carrying leaves and small branches along.

"I don't know what I'm supposed to be looking at. It's just a creek," Thomas admitted.

"Describe it to me. Pretend I'm blind. Don't leave out a single feature," Father Dominic suggested.

Thomas stared at the water again, wondering where to begin.

"Well, let's see. There's a lot of water in the creek today. It's running really high. There are more rapids than usual, and there's a part upstream, just before it bends out of sight, where the water is almost still. You can see the reflection of the trees and sky there. It's probably really deep there. Might be a good spot for fishing. Downstream the noise the water makes seems louder, like maybe the current picks up down that way or something," Thomas explained slowly, wondering if there was anything he might have left out.

"That's a good start, but you're missing quite a few details," Father Dominic said.

Thomas assessed the river once more, turning his attention to the bank leading down to the water's edge. It looked steep and slick.

"Well, there's a few big branches that are kinda sticking out of the water up to the right of us. And there's grass growing along most of the bank, some of it goes right down to the water where the bank doesn't slope as steep. Down the ways a bit, where the water starts getting rough, I could probably get down to the water there," Thomas concluded.

"Ah…yes…the bank," Father Dominic nodded, smiling at Thomas to encourage him further. "That's a good place to start. Every river has a bank, well, two actually, yes? What else have we missed?"

"Like what, how the water feels? I'd have to go down there and touch it. I'm not sure I want to risk it," Thomas admitted.

"So…is that it?" Father Dominic asked.

"Yeah, I think so. Why? What do you see?" Thomas probed inquisitively.

"I still don't know where the river begins, or where it ends. I don't know where it comes from, or where it goes. I don't know what it looked like yesterday, or what it will look like tomorrow," Father Dominic put forth.

"How the heck am I supposed to see all that?"

Father Dominic smiled, his body shaking slightly as he silently laughed.

"Exactly, Thomas. Exactly. Now, think of your life as this river. If I were to ask you to describe it to me, how much of your life would you be able to share?"

This was a question Thomas had never thought about before. Considering his life like this felt strange, uncomfortable.

"I guess I'd share just about as much. I'd only talk about the part I understand now. I guess I'd only tell you about what I know," Thomas offered.

"Precisely my point, Thomas. You see, your life is just like this river. The banks of this river determine its boundaries, how far it can stray from one side to another. Your life has boundaries as well, does it not?" Father Dominic questioned.

"What kind of boundaries?" Thomas asked.

"Well, for one, where you live now is a boundary. It might not be where you want to live, and it's not where you lived before the retreat, but for now, this is where you are. Oh sure, you could run away, go join a circus or something. But if you did, you wouldn't eliminate your boundaries, you would just move them. You can't be in more than one place at one time, just like you can't be more than one person at the same time. Your boundaries prevent that.

"There are simply some things about life you can't change. Like this river here before us. It flows only within the banks that define its existence. Sure, the river could swell so high that it crests over the tops of the banks, the water flooding out, spreading wherever it could. But the banks would still be here. Floods don't last forever. Eventually, the river would return to its banks, even though those banks might be different after the flood.

"And, like this river, you don't know where your life came from. Sure, you have memories about some of it, important events in life, things your brain decided you might need later on. But you can no longer see your origin. Neither can you see your destination. You don't know where this river flows from here once it passes beyond that bend downstream. We can guess what might be down there, but we don't know for sure unless we go down there to see.

"And, like this river, your life has had some very deep, still moments, like your experience on the retreat. I'm thinking your life felt pretty calm and tranquil after that experience. Like you had figured everything out, correct?"

Thomas nodded. "Yeah, you can say that. But that didn't last long. Watching the water go from hardly moving to crashing over rocks is kinda like what my life has done these past few months."

"Are you sure the water isn't moving in the part where it's smooth? Or is it moving underneath, where we can't see it?" Father Dominic asked.

Thomas looked again at the calm pool of water.

"I guess, if you think about it, the water has to be moving just as fast. We just can't see it, because it's so deep. It's running under the surface."

"My boy, you are a smart one. It takes some people much longer to figure this out!" Father Dominic said proudly, flashing Thomas a wide grin.

"So, what does all this have to do with the fight I had today? How does all that fit in?" Thomas asked.

"What is the one thing you know for sure about this river? Regardless if the water is smooth or full of rapids. Regardless if the river is shallow or deep. Regardless if the bank is steep, or if it slopes down gently. What is always the same? What's constant?" Father Dominic asked, sitting back slightly as he opened his arms out wide, gesturing at the swollen creek below.

Thomas stared intently at the water flowing below him. He turned his head to the right, examining the deep, still part of the river, focusing his attention on the gentle swirls that appeared, moved gracefully across the surface, and then disappeared once more. He watched as leaves and small branches floated across the mirror-like surface, spinning and twisting as they migrated between the swirls. Turning his head, he looked downstream towards the rapids, watching the water bubble up and down as it cascaded over the rocks below.

Looking back upstream, his attention was caught by two leaves drifting around the bend, bobbing softly in the gentle waves. One of the leaves got caught in a swirl that appeared underneath it. The leaf spun around again and again. The other leaf remained still, barely moving. The leaf that had been caught in the swirl broke free, bouncing between branches that were sticking up from the surface. The other leaf continued to glide effortlessly. Still, with all the variations in movement, they reached the beginning of the rapids at the same time. They had taken two different paths, but they arrived together.

He watched the leaves tumble and dance between the rocks. Sometimes they seemed to merge, swirling as one, dropping over and darting between the rapids. At other points, they were separate and unique. One leaf would race ahead, only to get stuck in a slower eddy, allowing the other to catch up. They would dance together again, then separate once more. He watched them until they disappeared around the bend, then turned, giving Father Dominic a look of comprehension.

"The constant is the flow. At times it appears to move slow and smooth, at times it looks like it moves fast and rough. But, the truth is, it is always flowing the same.

It doesn't matter what path the leaves and sticks take; eventually, they get where the river takes them. They can get stuck for a moment, but they always float free."

"Good for you, Thomas," Father Dominic beamed with pride, folding his hands in his lap. "You're right. The water flows where it does simply because it flows. It isn't good in some parts or bad in others; it's just different. It's all part of the flow. Just like life. Life itself is like this river, and we are like those leaves and sticks floating above. At times life feels like it slows down, allowing us to rest and reflect. At other times, it bounces along faster than we can keep up. As we float along, we don't know the origins of the river, or how it started. And we don't know where we will eventually end up. All we know is the part we are on. And like those two leaves you were watching, there is no one path down the river, just like there is not one path through life.

"We respond to the flow, move in the direction it carries us, spinning around, dancing through the waves, floating alone at times, and at other times we share our journey. Yet always, we flow."

Father Dominic paused, looking to gauge Thomas' understanding, and then continued on.

"There is one more thing we don't see; the water is constantly changing! It's never the same river twice. If you were to take a glass down to the river and fill it and then dump the water out again, it wouldn't matter how many times you tried, you could never capture that same water again. And yet, in all that change, it is still constant in its flow. Tenacious, one might say."

Father Dominic swatted at one of the many buzzing, flying insects that were rapidly growing in numbers, a good sign that the sun was beginning to set. He glanced at his watch and then nodded to himself as if in agreement with what he had seen there. Swatting once more, he turned back to face Thomas.

"An ancient Greek philosopher named Heraclitus once said, 'On those stepping into rivers staying the same, other and other waters flow,' which has been interpreted to mean 'One cannot step into the same river twice.' For, although the river seems constant, the fact is, it is always changing, always moving, always flowing.

"And, like the river, life flows. It moves. It changes. With each moment it is new, and yet, it is the same. And though we believe we are free, like those leaves you see floating by, we are always subject to the flow of life. Our one true freedom is not in our decision about what life will bring to us…"

Thomas interrupted, speaking softly, "We are only free in how we choose to respond."

Father Dominic sat up straight, a look of admiration and respect on his face.

"Yes, Thomas. We are only free in how we respond to life. In the slow, gentle parts of life, we can feel relieved, grateful for the chance to rest. Or we can feel agitated and upset, feeling like we aren't going anywhere, like we're stuck. In the rapids, we can feel desperate, frustrated, anxious, trying to find a moment of peace in what feels like an uncontrollable turbulence. Or we could choose to feel excited, daring, or even proud of how we withstand the rough waters. Life isn't about what's happening to us or around us…"

Once more Thomas finished Father Dominic's thought, "It's about how we feel about what's happening. It's about choosing our response, not choosing our path."

Father Dominic stood up, holding his hand.

"Come, Thomas. We should be getting back before the mosquitoes make us choose frustration," he laughed, swatting at another unseen foe.

Thomas accepted the outstretched hand, allowing Father Dominic to assist him up. He now understood that it's never a bad thing to accept help when offered or even to ask for help at times. Being honest about his feelings wasn't a sign of weakness. It was a sign of strength.

If he chose to feel angry about the situation with his dad, then that was his choice. He didn't have to explain why he chose to feel that way. His choice was his choice. It might not have been the best choice to make, but it wasn't a wrong one. The decision to feel angry, or sad, or to feel nothing at all, was his choice to make. All he had in life, where his true freedom lay, was in the knowledge and acceptance of this one truth. Life wasn't what it was until Thomas decided what it was. And that choice would always be his.

The two walked in silence along the path towards home. Thomas was deep in thought, and Father Dominic, aware of this, allowed Thomas the space needed to clarify his new insight. He knew what Thomas learned this afternoon would change everything about his life. From that point on, Thomas would never look at life the same.

As they walked, Thomas appreciated the quiet moment for reflection. He realized his old way of thinking would have left him feeling uncomfortable, afraid that he had done something wrong. But now, in this moment, he could see how many different options he had in front of him, how many emotions and responses he could choose. And he knew he chose the one that he did because that was how he wanted to feel. It was the choice that gave him the most peace.

As they approached the house, Father Dominic reached out and grasped Thomas' sleeve, stopping to share one last thought.

"What we did today, Thomas, is a process you can use at any time in life, whenever something comes along that you don't understand, or when you feel that there may be a deeper meaning to a situation. It's a process some refer to as Contemplative Prayer, a form of meditation. It can be used as easily as any prayer. Simply offer up a difficult situation to God, and then just observe how your mind and body respond. Always look for that one truth, however deep it may be buried.

"At times the process will feel liberating and free. Other times you'll be left with nothing. But that's not the point of Contemplative Prayer. Its purpose isn't to reach a destination, just like the purpose of the river isn't to reach whatever lake or larger river it merges with. The purpose is to be in the flow, to look at the situation with a new set of eyes, to hear with a different set of ears, to understand with a new way of thinking. The purpose of contemplation is to contemplate. What comes is what comes, understand?"

Thomas nodded his head. "Yeah, I get it. It's like anything else in life. It doesn't mean anything until I give it meaning."

"Good…good. Now, do you recall when we first started praying? I said we would pray to Our Lady of Mount Carmel." Father Dominic inquired, releasing his hold on Thomas' arm as he began walking once more.

"Yeah, sure," Thomas replied.

"Well, you see, long before I was a Franciscan, I was very much attracted to the Order of Carmelites, primarily for their devotion to this process of contemplation.

It's a very different way of living than what most people are used to, and it can take some time to really master it. But if you are open to it, I'll send you some books that might help. The way you caught on to it today, I think this will be of great help for you, especially in those moments when you feel you have nowhere else to turn. Or when you feel like you're about to go into Hulk mode," he said, winking at Thomas.

"You can use contemplation with major decisions in life, like asking God to help you find your purpose. Or you can use it to overcome areas of life where you feel stuck. It can help get to the true root of the issue, allowing you to find forgiveness and peace. In fact, in some ways, we are always using contemplation. For example, when you pick between two possible choices, like which breakfast cereal you want to eat, or choose what to order at a restaurant, or pick out what music you feel like listening to. All of these are very quick, very simple choices that we spend just a tiny amount of time contemplating. Does this make sense?"

"I never thought about it like that before, but yeah, it does. And yes, please do send me the books. I liked what we did today and would like to try it again," Thomas responded, wishing he had known about contemplation earlier in the day.

"Well, then, check your mailbox in a week or so. I'll send them here for you right away."

Thomas smiled, and then, seeing they had made it back to the Thompson's yard, stopped suddenly as a new realization came to him. He grabbed Father Dominic's arm, preventing him from going any further.

"Father, if you wouldn't mind. Can you go in by yourself? There's something I need to do."

Father Dominic smiled knowingly.

"Of course. Will you be long?"

"I shouldn't be, no. Just a minute or two."

Father Dominic nodded gently, then turned away, walking the rest of the way alone. Thomas watched until Father Dominic was securely in the house, and then made his way around the side to the front yard. Across the driveway from the front door, there was a stone bench sitting in the middle of a paved path, surrounded by flowers and shrubs. He took a seat facing the house and began to just look. Though his eyes focused outward, his mind was focused within.

He contemplated his feelings about calling this place 'home'. He knew, deep inside, he never made the choice to surrender to this part of life. He was trying to swim against the current, struggling to make things different than they were. And because of that, he suffered. He saw how his decision to feel distant and unattached to this house was exactly why he was feeling distant and unattached to Ben and Terri, why he didn't feel like anything that he had here was 'his,' why he felt that he didn't belong. And in that moment, he contemplated a different way of being.

Thomas stood and walked to the front door. He paused just for a moment, his thumb resting on the lever that would release the lock. Then, slowly, he pressed it down. The tell-tale 'click' penetrated deep into his soul as he swung the door open and walked inside. For the first time since moving into the Thompson's house more than eight months ago, Thomas was home.

# PART TWO

*We can't have full knowledge all at once. We must
start by believing; then afterwards we may be led.*
                                        *— St. Thomas Aquinas*

# INTERLUDE
## THERESA

"Forty-two more hours…" Theresa thought as she looked around the yurt she had been assigned, spotting a lone bed at the back corner; if a yurt had corners, that is. Yurts were a more permanent form of a tent, with canvas walls and roof stretched around a fixed wooden structure. They were typically round, yet the placement of furniture inside this one gave the illusion of square-ness. Each of the yurts had accommodations for eleven, with five sets of bunk beds and one single bed. Theresa had chosen the single bed for two reasons. First, it was the furthest away from the door and in the most secluded spot in the tent. And second, because the rest of the giggling, hyperactive, attention-craving girls in her yurt had already split into pairs by the time the bus had left the church parking lot. Now all they had to decide was who got the top bunk.

That was fine with her. She was used to being left alone. In fact, she preferred blending into the background. Most days she wanted nothing more than to disappear. There had been a few times where she had done exactly that, too. Disappear, that is. She was getting pretty good at it. This weekend would be a good way to test just how far her powers reached. And so, as the lip-gloss sharing, perfume-laden, selfie-taking, Twitter-ites around her hugged and posed and giggled even more, she slipped through them, drawing no more attention than a whisper. She moved to the lone bed in the back corner, and quietly set down her things.

"Forty-two more hours..." she repeated as two of the girls began gathering the others for a group picture on the bunk bed in the center of the room. She wasn't sure she could make it that long. Outside the yurt, Theresa could hear Amanda, the Youth Minister for her church, as she went from yurt to yurt, calling out role. Inside, the desire to test her burgeoning powers continued to nag at her mind. She knew if she didn't respond when her name was called, Amanda would start a search of the campgrounds to find her. Theresa's mom had checked her in when she dropped her off at the bus, so there was no reason Theresa shouldn't be here now.

Amanda appeared in the doorway, rattling off one name after another as the others responded with loud, high-pitched squeals. When the others had all responded and Amanda started to turn to leave, Theresa realized her name hadn't been called. Taking a risk, she looked towards Amanda, wondering if perhaps she had truly disappeared. Amanda had stopped at the doorway and was staring at her clipboard as if there was something wrong, but she couldn't figure out just what.

"Wait a minute. There's supposed to be eleven in each yurt..." she said, her voice trailing off.

Looking back up to count heads, Amanda turned her head in the direction where Theresa stood. Their eyes connected just briefly, but that was enough.

"Oh...Theresa. Didn't I call your name?"

Theresa shook her head as she stepped forward, causing one of her yurt-mates to jump.

"Oh, geez! Didn't even see you there!" the girl exclaimed, dropping her selfie stick.

Amanda turned her attention back to her list, checking off the eleventh name in Yurt number five.

"Dinner is in five minutes, girls," Amanda announced. "That's five…not ten! I had to make special arrangements for us to eat this late."

With that, Amanda moved on to the next yurt in the cluster of tents, and the girls in Theresa's yurt resumed their giggling.

"I'm Megan," said the girl who had jumped when Theresa had stepped forward. Then, with a look of realization, she reached down for her selfie stick, adding, "Oh crap, you weren't in the group selfie! Hey guys, we gotta do the shot again. Theresa wasn't in it!" she shouted, a little louder than necessary.

Theresa cringed inside. The absolute last thing she wanted was to appear in a photo. Once the camera captured her image, there would be proof she was here, and her invisibility wouldn't work for a time, perhaps the entire weekend. She couldn't let that happen.

"That's okay, maybe later. I think I heard Amanda say we need to get to dinner."

"Okay, whatever," Megan shot back with disdain.

The ten girls left the yurt in pairs, arms linked or holding hands, leaving Theresa alone for a moment. She waited a moment or two more to ensure there would be distance between her and her yurt-mates and then headed out the door. On the way to the dining hall, she went through her checklist to help engage her power.

*Don't look anyone in the eye.*
*Don't make any sudden moves.*
*Don't do anything stupid.*
*Don't attract attention.*
*Don't trip.*
*Don't bump anyone.*
*Don't cough.*

Theresa did her best to slip into the line of teens without anyone noticing, though she could tell something just wasn't right. The feeling she usually had when she was invisible wasn't there. Her power wasn't working. Perhaps she had unknowingly caught someone's attention. Though she wanted to know if that was the case, she couldn't look up. If she had, and their eyes met, she would be back to square one. Theresa simply held her gaze on the red plastic tray in her hands, moving slowly forward in the sea of hungry teens.

As she was about to reach out and grab what looked like an especially good cornbread muffin, she heard the boy standing behind her say, "Dang...only one muffin left! Who wants to fight for it?"

Theresa had been so focused on trying to disappear, she hadn't noticed she was about to take the last one. Fear gripped her as she realized, had she done so, the boy behind her would definitely have noticed, perhaps even resented her. That would have given him a reason to look for her, again and again, all weekend. Perhaps he would even point her out to his friends. Slowly, she pulled back her hand, leaving the muffin where it was. In that moment of sacrifice, she felt the world slip away. A smile came across her lips as she realized she had done it. She had once more disappeared.

# CHAPTER NINE
## MORNING PRAYERS

The morning fog whispered peacefully between the massive trunks of the redwood trees as the teens made their way from breakfast to the chapel for Morning Prayer. Brother Thomas stood in the midst of a small copse of trees, the only spot within walking distance from the dining hall where the sun had broken through. Below him, at the bottom of a steep bank choked with vegetation, a creek flowed noiselessly by. Instantly, Thomas was transported back to a warm, summer day four years ago, the day Father Dominic had taken him to the river behind the Thompson's house. The day he had learned the lesson of life by contemplating a river.

A lot had changed over those years. His mom eventually came out of her coma, only a few months into his junior year. After a couple of weeks of physical therapy, she was released, finally able to return home. Thomas remembered how hard he had cried that day, standing once more in his old bedroom, smelling once more the familiar scent of home. He still kept in touch with the Thompson's, staying at their house occasionally over long weekends, especially when Lily was there.

His relationship with Ben and Terri had changed that afternoon as well, as he began to choose his response to life, rather than letting his emotions choose for him. It was still hard. There were plenty of days when he gave up fighting and just let his emotions win. Luckily those days didn't come as often anymore.

His relationship with Julianna had improved as he had once more found the ability to offer her the support and comfort she needed. He showed her how to use contemplative prayer to help her understand the challenges of her own life, and together they would spend hours just sitting in the backyard, contemplating life.

Julianna was becoming a strong, dynamic young woman, and had started making choices to change her life for the better. She had changed the group of friends she had had since grade school, deciding that worrying about fashion and popularity was no longer who she wanted to be. Instead, she chose a group of friends who were more practical, relaxed, and openly honest with each other.

The same held true for Thomas' relationship with Lily. Though he still loved her deeply, his love for her no longer came from desire, but from total acceptance of who she was. Shortly after she had returned from Europe, he had told her of his intentions to enter the priesthood and asked for her support. Their conversation that night went long into the morning hours, but they came out of it two different people. Gone were the fantasies of their youth, replaced with an undying commitment to always be there for each other, no matter what. Their friendship became wholesome, unshakeable, and eternal.

The biggest surprise, however, was his relationship with his father. The anger and pain he felt for his dad had been replaced with deep feelings of compassion and mercy. He knew he couldn't control the way his dad behaved any more than he could the weather. Instead, he decided to rise above his fear. Rather than challenge his dad to take responsibility for every wrong thing his father had ever done, he told him he forgave him for all that had happened. His father had acted as if the words meant nothing, but Thomas knew that they had. He had learned to see beyond the surface of others emotions, to look deep into someone's eyes and see the current moving beneath their storms.

A few weeks after his father was released from jail, his dad had moved away, refusing to have anything to do with the family anymore. Thomas didn't know where his father had gone but had decided it wasn't his concern. His dad had his own path to follow. It was up to Thomas to just accept him for who he was. What effect their final conversation had on his father, Thomas may never know, but he was okay with that. He had begun to understand the value in letting things go. Plus, Thomas knew the effect that conversation with his father had had for himself. He knew forgiving someone was never meant so the other person would feel better, but so the one granting forgiveness would find peace.

Telling his father that he still loved him despite everything created a space in his heart Thomas hadn't known existed before. It was within that space that Thomas had found an even greater desire to enter spiritual life. With the help of Father Dominic and a generous donation from the Thompson's, he was accepted by the Franciscan University of Steubenville, where he was now working towards a Masters in Divinity. He was in the second half of his sophomore year, coming home to pay back a long overdue debt. He had once made a promise to Amanda that he would repay her for everything she had done for him. This seemed like as good of a time as any.

Now, as the sound of laughter filled the air, Thomas began focusing his thoughts in preparation for the day. He looked out among the trees and buildings surrounding the small copse where he stood, noticing the changes the facility had gone through since the last time he was here. It definitely had a new coat of paint. He didn't recall the buildings looking so bright. Most of the paths had been paved over as well, permanently removing the footprints he had left in the dirt during his frantic rush across these grounds.

Reflecting on his own life, he realized the changes he had experienced within far outnumbered any of those on the outside. Although he still looked a lot like that same young, somewhat shy kid who had very little interest in anything spiritual or religious four years ago, he knew nothing could be further from the truth.

However, there was one exterior change that had taken place to distinguish him from his younger self. Over the typical clothes he normally wore, he now draped the tunic, hood, and cord of the Third Order of Franciscans. He also now went by the title of Brother Thomas, a name he would carry until he completed his formal education and entered the formation process required to finally be a priest.

He liked that he already looked like a priest, although it was difficult at times when people who didn't know him yet would call him Father. And there were still certain religious functions that he could not yet perform. But at least with his current status, he was able to participate more formally in the lifestyle of the religious order. It gave him a different perspective, especially in the way the youth responded to him on this retreat.

For fun, he had performed a small test on Friday night when the teens arrived. He left his tunic and hood in his cabin and just hung out like he was one of the many other young adults Amanda normally recruited to help out. He ate with them, joked with them, talked the same language, and even participated in the ice breaker games as if he was still just Thomas, which, in truth, was all he really believed he was, even with the new title.

After the icebreakers, the participants were separated into their small groups, and Amanda began to introduce the ministry team for the weekend. Thomas had stepped outside, put on his tunic and hood, and waited just outside the door for her to call his name. When she introduced 'Brother Thomas', he walked back in, a huge smile on his face. As he entered the room, he could see the look of surprise on most of the teens faces. A few, though, looked embarrassed, perhaps recalling conversations that had taken place earlier that evening, wondering if they needed to apologize for something they might have said.

Brother Thomas told those in the room not to worry. Underneath his tunic, he was still just like them, just a few years older. He explained the difference between a brother and a priest, letting them know he was available for the weekend to provide spiritual guidance or counseling, but he was unable to hear confession, or perform other duties reserved solely for priests. One of his biggest responsibilities would be leading prayer, which brought his thoughts back to what he was about to accomplish this morning.

He thought about some of the teens he had already met, and others he had made mental notes to make sure he got to know. He had identified a few who he could tell were on the retreat because their parents made them come. Thomas knew there was an even larger group that, though they had come because they wanted to, it was not for the spiritual formation the weekend would provide. Instead, this group came simply for the chance to get away from home. The smallest group, and the one least noticeable, would be the few, burning, passionate hearts belonging to those who had already come to know and understand their faith.

Standing in this small space of warmth, surrounded by the morning fog and dew soaked trees, Brother Thomas knew finding this final, passionate group would be his focus this weekend. Giving them permission to open up, to share the depths of their faith with the rest of the teens would be the key to leaving here with more believers than had arrived last night. He knew some of those who were currently on the fence about anything church related might be willing to open their hearts just a little more if they saw some of their peers doing the same. And so, he prayed. He asked God to help him stand in the midst of those few faithful hearts, just as he stood within this small group of trees. And he asked God to help him feel their faith burning within them the same as he felt the heat of the sun reflecting off the bark of these trees.

At that moment, the clouds shifted, temporarily blocking the sun. A gentle reminder of how fragile the relationship of faith can be. Thomas felt an inner connection to the warmth as it passed, sensing that his own faith was as transient as vapors in the wind if not constantly warmed by Jesus' light. It wasn't that he didn't believe in the church, or that he no longer felt like a Christian. It was much deeper than that. Perhaps it came from old wounds reaching up towards the surface, or from reaching a point in life where things had once more become mundane and predictable. Or perhaps it was simply the memories of how he had felt the first time he had come to this retreat center, how distant and aloof his faith was back then. Wherever they came from, he no longer felt sure he was where he was supposed to be.

Brother Thomas placed his hand on the tree nearest his side, feeling the lingering presence of warmth still clutching to the bark. Smiling to himself, he lifted his hand and stepped away, taking one last deep, penetrating breath, holding on to the peace he felt within. He released his breath in a slow, controlled sigh, trying to send his doubts along with it as best he could. He knew that the true work of this weekend was already in God's hands, he was just the messenger. Reaching into his pocket, he withdrew his rosary beads, then headed towards the chapel to lead the teens in prayer.

Thomas walked the path from the dining hall to the chapel in silence, letting the 'skiff' sounds made as his tunic dragged across the concrete path be the only sound he heard. Guided by the somewhat hypnotic rhythm, his thoughts drifted deeper, past the surface fears and doubts that floated above like so much flotsam, allowing him to let go more fully as he walked along. He approached the door to the chapel, pausing just a moment. His thoughts flashed back to that morning seemingly so far away, and yet not that long ago. That morning four years ago when he had stumbled recklessly through this very portal, crashing heavily on the hardwood floor, waking up to find Father Dominic there to help lead him home.

In many ways, that morning reminded him of the nativity story, as his own faith life had been born here in this chapel. Focusing on the birth of Christ reminded Thomas of how God had chosen the simplest way to bring His presence into the world. This gave him hope that he would find the same for his own faith. In a similar way, Thomas hoped he would one day simply wake up to find, within the small manger of his heart, his Savior would now reside.

Inside the chapel, the teens had gathered and were seated in groups of three or four; spread out on the floor between the pews, around the altar, anywhere they felt comfortable. On one side of the altar, the music ministry team was quietly playing, setting the tone for this first session of the day. He knew praying the rosary would be uncomfortable for those who had never learned formal prayers, or perhaps had never even heard their parents praying out loud. It was these teens that his heart went out to the most. They reminded him of where he had come from, and how far he still had to go.

Brother Thomas looked around the room, watching the youth interact with each other. He also took note of how the young adults were connecting with the groups they had chosen to join. He saw two youth and one young adult who had not joined a group but instead sat alone. All three seemed to be deep in prayer, two with heads bowed low, and the third with her face cast up to the cross. He made a mental note of these three, knowing he would want to catch each of them alone at some point this weekend. These were some of those elusive, passionate hearts he was in search of, those he knew held the key to his success.

Amanda motioned him over to where she sat, reviewing the plan for the prayer session with the lead of the music team. Together the three talked quietly about what was to come.

"Good morning, Brother," Amanda greeted him.

"Hello, Amanda. How are you today?" he replied.

"As good as can be expected. Nervous, excited, ready for whatever God has planned!"

"Good morning Brother," Stephen added, "Any special requests for the music today?"

Thomas shook his head.

"I'll follow your lead. Just keep it gentle and flowing. Nothing familiar. I think it might be best for their minds to focus on the prayer instead of the songs."

Stephen nodded. "Sounds good. I've got a few new songs we've worked on that we haven't introduced at Youth Group yet. Those should work."

Amanda nodded in agreement, then turned to look back at Brother Thomas.

"Whenever you're ready," she said, giving him one of her confident, trusting smiles.

Taking another deep breath, Thomas raised his right hand high overhead, a signal for the group to quiet down and give him their attention. Slowly, as one teen after another saw his signal and raised their own hands high, the silence spread.

"Good morning, my friends. I hope you all slept at least a few hours last night," Brother Thomas began.

They replied with greetings back, some of them turning to smile knowingly at a friend. It wasn't uncommon for the teens to spend most of the first night up late talking in their cabins or sneaking out for a moonlit hike.

"Just out of curiosity, how many here have prayed the rosary before?" he asked.

Almost every hand in the room went up. Having been in Amanda's program himself as a teen, Thomas knew she had at least one rosary prayer session every few months. It wasn't a shock to see many hands raised.

"Well then, good job Amanda!" he said, turning and nodding in appreciation to the Youth Minister. "Okay, so, next question. How many of you, outside of Youth Group, have ever taken the time to pray the rosary on your own?"

Stephen, Amanda, about half of the music team, most of the young adult volunteers, and three teens raised their hands. Of the three teens, two of them were those Brother Thomas had seen silently praying when he entered the room.

"For those of you whose hands are down, is there a reason you haven't taken the time to learn and practice this prayer? Now, don't answer. Let me tell you what I've heard from others and see if this applies to you. First, they say they can never find the time. Yet, most of us find the time to watch our favorite TV shows, listen to music, play video games, or any other number of activities that do little to help develop spiritual warriors."

He raised both arms above his head, flexing as he imagined a body builder might as he said these last words. This brought a small amount of laughter from the group and even more silent smiles.

"Now, I don't recommend you rush through the prayers, but if you had to because of time, you could complete them in about ten or fifteen minutes. So, finding time isn't really a valid excuse, is it?"

The response was a mix, some bowing their heads in recognition that he was probably right, others shaking their heads in agreement.

"Next, I've heard people say they don't always carry their rosary with them, and they can't remember all of the prayers. Who here would honestly consider praying the rosary more often if they didn't have to carry the rosary with them?"

A few hands went up.

"Okay, good, good. That's a start. I've made a list of apps, for both the iPhone and Android. We will hand it out at the end of the retreat, at the same time that you will get your phones back. That way, you can load one or two of the apps right away, before you get distracted by the real world. Sound good?"

As he spoke, he was looking specifically for anyone who turned their eyes away from him at that question. He knew anyone who wouldn't keep his gaze was either on the fence about their faith, or they had absolutely no interest in deepening their faith at all. Another few faces were logged in his memory for follow-up conversations throughout the weekend.

"So the final reason why people don't pray is that they don't *understand* the prayers. So let me explain. These prayers are more than just repeating memorized words, over and over. They are a deeply contemplative exercise, a way of truly looking inside our hearts, examining how we feel about the symbolism of each decade as we pray.

"So, I'm going to tell you what I would like from you for this prayer today, although it's up to you to follow through or not," Thomas said, pausing until he had the attention of the entire room. "Surrender any doubts, or fears, or uncomfortable feelings you might have about the rosary, and just keep this one thought in mind. When you stand on the beach, looking out at the ocean, what do you see?"

He paused, waiting for a response.

"The waves," came a response from somewhere behind him.

"Exactly," Thomas said, turning in the direction of the voice. "One wave after another, crashing into the shore. Majestic, sure, but it can also be repetitive, monotonous, even boring. Well, here's the thing. What you see is only a small portion of what the ocean truly is. The shorelines of all the beaches in all the world only make up

the smallest percentage of the entire ocean. To really experience the ocean, you have to leave the shore. You have
to abandon what is safe and familiar. You need to sail out
to where you've never been before.

"And when you get out there, you'll find that it
looks very, very different. Yes, there are still waves, but
instead of just moving in one direction, they seem to come
from everywhere, sometimes all at once. At times, the
waves are gentle, barely noticeable. At other times, the sea
can rise and fall with a viciousness that can scare even the
most experienced sailor. But even in the middle of the
ocean, we are only looking at a small percent of the ocean
as a whole. Does anyone know why?"

A longer pause, this time with no response.

"Because we are only looking at the surface. Beneath the waves, the ocean is a completely different
world. It doesn't matter what's going on at the surface,
underneath it is always gentle and calm, peaceful. This is
where you want to go when we pray the rosary."

A few heads nodded, but no one looked away.

"Just like going out to sea gives us a different view
of the ocean, contemplative prayer gives us a new way of
experiencing our faith. Now, I want you to picture your
mind like that ocean, way out there, out where you can no
longer see the shore. Your thoughts are the waves. They
come from every direction, crashing into each other.
Sometimes your mind is quiet and still, and you feel
peaceful inside. Other times, your thoughts come so fast
and so powerful, the storm inside your head can scare the
crap out of you. Who's been there before?"

Although he saw a less physical acknowledgment
of what he was saying, Brother Thomas could see understanding shining back from the eyes in front of him.

"So, during this prayer, your mind may be gentle and calm, or it might be rough and turbulent, tossing around, out of control. The point isn't to try and calm your mind. If it's out of control, let it be. The point is to dive down under the surface, to find the calm beneath the waves. When we pray the rosary, the repeated prayers are what happens on the surface. They are there to distract our thoughts while our minds dive deep below.

"What we are doing while we dive, is using the images our minds create to draw us even further down. As we hear the scriptures before each decade, we want our attention to go beneath the waves, down into our hearts. We want to contemplate the life of our brother Jesus, our Mother Mary, and what they mean to us. So, during this prayer, number one, please don't distract your neighbor. If this prayer isn't your thing, that's okay. Pray along with us if you choose, or simply sit quietly and think about what your faith means to you. If you don't think it means anything at all, that's okay too. Give yourself this time to contemplate why it doesn't mean anything, or what would have to change for you to let it mean something. And let your neighbor have this time as well, agreed?"

A chorus of 'yes' responses came back, some verbal, some not.

"Thank you. Oh, and one last thing. There is no right way or wrong way to hold the rosary," he said, lifting up his own rosary. "This is simply a tool to help you know where you are in the prayer process. We follow it, one bead at a time, as we repeat each prayer. If you get lost, look up at the screen behind the altar. We are going to show you what one of the apps looks like, and Amanda will have it follow along with us as we pray. This way, you can get a feel of what using those apps might be like, and so you will know where you are supposed to be on the beads. As you become more familiar with the rosary, you'll get better at being in the right place."

He turned to Amanda, checking to ensure she was ready. She gave him a thumbs up, silently mouthing "That was awesome!"

He grinned back at her. He knew the words didn't come from him. Spirit was starting to move within this retreat. Like the rosary in the hands of the teens, he saw himself as a tool in the process of whatever plan God had in store.

"Okay, then, let's begin. We start with the normal blessing. In the name of the Father…"

About a half-hour later, as the final words of the last prayer of the rosary echoed in the rafters of the chapel, Brother Thomas could feel a presence within the room. The faces of those he could see reflected back a deep sense of peace. He had taken them below the surface, well, most of them anyway. There were a few whose faces looked so peaceful, he thought it may be possible they had fallen asleep. Such was the challenge of youth ministry retreats.

He let the silence hang for a moment, letting the peacefulness of the prayers float throughout the room. As the eyes of the teens began to open up again, he quietly addressed the room.

"Now, that was one of the best morning rosary prayers I've experienced. I can tell some of you went far beneath the waves, yes? It's evident in the stillness in the room. Can you feel it? Just sit for a moment as your minds come back, hold on to that peace we shared for just a moment longer."

Brother Thomas paused again, watching as flickers of warmth, like small tongues of fire, began to dance above the heads of those in the room. Though it had been some time since he had last seen any of these curious, emotionally charged shapes, he had learned to welcome them when they did come. Or at least, to not resist. This time, he was glad they were there, as they reflected back to him the same feeling he had inside his own heart.

"One of the most important things you can learn to do while you're still teens," he continued, "and one of the things that helped me get through one of the biggest struggles in my life was to find time to enter into stillness like we did today. Your worlds are so full of noise, so distracting. Let's give ourselves the gift today of holding on to this moment as long as we can."

Brother Thomas turned to the music team, whispering, "Play something gentle and quiet."

Stephen nodded back, turning to give his musicians a few directions. The pianist began first, playing softly. The guitar came in next with a gentle picking pattern, followed by the choir, using 'ooh' or 'ah' instead of words. As they entered the chorus, Brother Thomas recognized the song. It was one he had learned during his freshman year at college. He had first heard it during a seminar he had taken during a youth ministry conference. The seminar focused on the effective use of music within a youth ministry program, and the presenter had offered this song as an example. The song was called *This Is Our Room*, written by Jesse Manibusan, a recording artist who had spent a large amount of his career working with youth. Though Thomas couldn't recall the words to the verses, the chorus had stuck with him ever since, and the words began to trickle through his mind.

*This is our room*
*These are our lives*
*We have courage to move*
*We have courage to rise*

The song floated back into the verse, and his mind floated gently back into thoughts about his ministry. He wondered if he truly had the courage to move, to stand against injustice in all areas of life, to grant forgiveness to all who asked. When it came to it, and he was asked to be Christ for another, would he have the courage to rise? His ears picked up the gentle sound of weeping coming from someone close to him. These teens who walked in last night, closed off and reserved, concerns for what they might experience weighing heavily in the backs of their minds, were already beginning to open up, letting their souls be revealed. This is why he loved Youth Ministry.

He couldn't see exactly who it was, so he whispered a blessing for the entire group, asking God to grant them bravery to face whatever fears they held inside, and to comfort any sense of loss or remorse in their hearts. He was about to stand back up and draw the session to a close when the music came back to the chorus once more. Inspired, he began to sing along, softly at first.

He glanced at Stephen, waving slightly to catch his attention. When he did, he rotated his index finger in small circles, hoping Stephen took the sign to keep playing the chorus. Stephen smiled and nodded, going back to the chorus a second time. Thomas continued to sing, his voice growing stronger. A few of the band members joined in. Turning slightly, he glanced over at Amanda, watching her typing furiously on her laptop. She looked up and caught his eye, giving him a broad smile. A moment later, the words for the chorus were up on the screen behind him. Thomas smiled, feeling a warmth flow across the room.

Without being asked, the teens began to follow Thomas' lead, singing softly at first, the words themselves propelling everyone to sing. This *was* their room…at least for this weekend. And these were their lives, broken and shared with as much reverence and honor as any Eucharistic celebration he had participated in, perhaps more than some. The music increased in volume as Stephen brought in the drums. A few of the more reluctant youth in the room began to at least mouth the words, while the rest were singing aloud.

Brother Thomas smiled. He knew this was where Youth Ministry happened. It didn't happen because it was part of the schedule, or because it had been planned. It was in spontaneous moments like these; in the chaos, the unforeseen, the space where spirit moved. Youth Ministry wasn't structured and organized. To an outsider, it probably looked messy and confused, but when it came down to it, it never mattered how many hours were spent planning, how many times the skits were rehearsed, or how perfect the talks were written. No one but God knew which moments would be the most powerful, which person would be touched by which talk, or what moments would create Holy Ground for His work to take place.

During the last repetition of the chorus, Brother Thomas stood up, followed by several others. More joined each moment. He looked around at the clusters of teens standing together, arms wrapped around each other, some with tears streaming down their face. They sang these simple words with such passion. He knew they would never have reached this point if they had been handed the lyrics on a page and asked to sing. They sang because they heard in these words their own desire to be in a relationship with Christ, to find a place they could feel this safe and comfortable in every moment of their frenzied life. Here, deep in these woods, far from the comforts and distractions of their homes, they were responding to God's call.

He looked over to see Amanda standing with her arms draped around two adult volunteers. Their eyes met for a moment, sharing a soundless "Yes!" She gave him a fist pump in recognition of what they both knew was happening. This was the point of every retreat that Youth Ministers from every church hope they can reach. A moment where those leading the retreat realize their task is complete. These teens, who came in cautious and reserved, had dropped their defenses, allowing themselves to become vulnerable. Here, so early into the weekend, too. This was special.

He turned to the music group, nodding his thanks to Stephen, whispering, "One more time." Stephen gestured to his musicians. One by one the instruments faded out, leaving only the piano. They played the chorus one last time, the piano fading away softly, finishing the song a cappella. More than ninety voices sounded together, harmoniously declaring that this room where they now stood had become Holy Ground.

# CHAPTER TEN
## AUDIBLES AND ADDICTIONS

The rest of the day progressed as planned. Brother Thomas spent most of his time watching as the teens shared during the large group discussions. From what he had witnessed, the small group conversations had been more than genuine as well. During the breaks, a few teens had sought him out, asking questions related to the discussions they had just had in their groups. Most of those questions were ones he had heard from others at this age: what the church taught about same-sex relationships, premarital sex, divorce and so forth. Very few rose from deep wounds or a longing desire for wisdom but from more of a casual observance of the discord between the message of the Gospel and what others had told them the church taught.

For the most part, what they had heard had originated from one of their friends, or more frequently, from the media. He shared what he knew about these topics, typically pulling out a copy of the YouCat, a teen version of the Catechism. As they researched the topic together, he kept an eye on their expression, looking for signs of possible deeper questions they were reluctant to express.

He had also kept his promise to find those teens he had made mental notes to connect with throughout the weekend. Those conversations were somewhat more engaging, and he felt positive about the results achieved. Now, he was about to have dinner with one more, a young woman his age named Beth. He had been watching her interact with the teens, noticing how easy it was for her to connect. She had a special way about her and was just as comfortable with the louder, more vivacious teens as she was with the introspective, thoughtful ones. When speaking with those in the exuberant group, she had a way of focusing their thoughts, drawing them in. She did the opposite with the contemplative teens, drawing them out from behind the introverted, shy masks they wore.

Perhaps out of comfort, Thomas had selected the same table where he and Father Dominic had held their conversation at lunch four years ago. As the two settled their trays upon the table, Beth immediately opened up.

"So, Brother Thomas, that was pretty cool this morning. I really liked that analogy about the ocean and our minds. So many times I feel like I'm going crazy in my head with all the thoughts crashing in," she admitted.

"Thanks, Beth. I have to give credit to Father Dominic, though. Most of that talk was one he gave a few years back. Do you know him?"

"I met him once, but I've only been a parishioner here for about a year. I used to live on the other side of town. But St. Matt's is closer to my apartment than my old church, so I switched," she told him.

"What made you move?" he inquired, casually spinning a fork-full of spaghetti.

"I reached a point where I was ready to be on my own, so I got a job that pays enough to afford an apartment. I share it with two other girls I know from school."

"What's that like?" Thomas asked.

"It's okay…mostly. Sometimes it sucks, though. Like how they're always leaving messes everywhere. Plus they're both in school, so to them, Friday nights are party nights. I usually work early on Saturdays," Beth sighed.

"Living with people can be a real test sometimes, I know. I've had two different roommates at college so far. The one I have this year is pretty nice, though," Thomas said, pausing for a moment as he took another bite. "So, where was it you said that you work?"

"I've got a paid internship at Project Rachel. Are you familiar with them?"

"No, I can't say that I am," Thomas confessed.

"They work with women who are dealing with the emotions of having an abortion. Mostly counseling stuff, which is what I really want to get into. I'm taking classes, online for now. I really want to work with young women in crisis. I feel like that's my calling in life, you know, like my purpose."

"Good to know. If anyone comes my way this weekend that I think you might be able to help, can I come find you?" Thomas asked.

"Oh, yeah! That would be perfect! I'd love to help wherever I can," Beth told him with an excited look.

The two went back to their meals for the moment, not realizing the agreement they had just entered into was part of a much larger plan for their lives, one that would further develop in just a few short hours. After dinner, he spent some time in his cabin reading through the Bible. One passage, in particular, caught his attention.

*More than that, we rejoice in our sufferings, knowing that suffering produces endurance, and endurance produces character, and character produces hope, and hope does not put us to shame because God's love has been poured into our hearts through the Holy Spirit who has been given to us.*
*– Romans 5:3-5*

Thomas thought back to the period of his life when he felt like he had suffered the most, considering how the trial he had undergone really had developed his character. Had he not gone through what he had, he might not have the same convictions or inner courage he felt now. Thomas considered how his previous, negative experiences had translated into hope, sensing that the strength he had developed was what was now providing him with the knowledge that, should he face similar challenges in the future, he could once again find his way through.

Opening the Bible once more, Thomas paused just a moment to check what time it was, realizing the dinner break had ended, and it was time to get back to the group. Marking the passage so he could continue reading later, he tucked the Bible under his arm and headed out the door. Walking back into the large conference room, Brother Thomas found Amanda in the middle of a conversation with a couple of the adult volunteers. Their eyes connected, and she motioned him over.

"Brother Thomas, how was dinner?" she asked.

"It was good, Amanda! Though I could use some of those red vines you always have on hand. I do believe they have become an addiction," he confessed.

"If you eat any more of those, we're going to have to start calling you Brother Red Vines!" Amanda joked, pointing to the snack table. "There's a jar over there. But come right back, we need to discuss the plan for tonight."

Thomas grabbed a dozen sticks, immediately tearing off a large section from three of the pieces. Satisfied they were fresh, he went back to join the group. Stephen turned towards him, pulling his hand out of his sweatshirt pocket, revealing his own stash. He winked at Thomas, sharing a moment of fraternity in their addiction.

"So, here's the situation," Amanda began when she had the group's attention. "We just lost one of our priests for reconciliation tonight, so I need to call an audible. With only one priest, it could take all night to get through confessions, and we just can't do that. At most, we can go two or three hours, which is what we planned with two priests. Now that Father Jim can't make it, we need a different plan."

Stephen's wife, Jennifer, offered a suggestion. "If it's a matter of making sure those teens who want to receive reconciliation are able to, then it would make sense to prevent kids going in who aren't interested in the Sacrament. Though it's our job to lead them to reconciliation when we can, since time is limited, I think we should focus on those that really want to go. We can always have another service when we get back to St. Matthew's sometime after the retreat. Plus, we usually get better participation from the surrounding parish priests."

"That's so true," Amanda agreed. "Two years ago we had a teen who took close to an hour and a half! The poor priest was completely drained. We can't let that happen again."

Brother Thomas offered, "Maybe we could set up a couple different rooms. Rather than set up the main room with two confessionals in the corners like we had planned, we could set up the main room for adoration. The music team can play some background music to keep the teens occupied. We can set up a private room in one of the small group rooms we are already using. Which priest did you say is still coming?"

"Father Jorge. He's already here and should be relaxing in his cabin," Amanda informed him, then turned to Stephen. "What do you think about this idea?"

"The band can definitely do the music. We've got a ton of good songs for adoration that we've been practicing lately, what with Lent coming up and all," Stephen shared.

"Okay, so that will at least give the teens something to do while they're waiting to meet with Father Jorge, but that doesn't shorten the amount of time it will take, even if we only have half the kids go. We still need something for those teens who want to talk to someone, but don't want to go to confession," Amanda stated.

"What if we set up a few other rooms?" Jennifer offered. "We could have some of the adults in them, not to hear confessions, but to be available to answer questions or just talk."

"That could work...but who do we put in those rooms?" Amanda asked.

"I could take one of them," Jennifer offered, "and Brother Thomas could take another. If we can find one more person, that should be enough."

"I've got to stay with the musicians," Stephen shared, reluctantly.

"And I can't step away for long," Amanda admitted, "I've got to coordinate everything here and be available if any issues come up in either of your rooms that would require me to report."

"Who are your two best young adult volunteers?" Thomas asked after a moment of silent consideration.

"Kevin has been around the program since he was in junior high. He's got a pretty good head on his shoulders. If I had to pick one more, it would probably be Kylie. She's a little shy at first, but she can come out of her shell when I need her to. Why? What do you have in mind?" Amanda inquired.

"What if we put them in charge of the large group, have them coordinate with the other young adults? They could field general questions here in this room, and you'll be in the room with them if they get stuck. If they get a question they can't answer, and the conversation would be too private for them to discuss with you in the large room, they can bring those teens to the rooms where Jennifer or I will be," Brother Thomas explained.

"And if the two of you get issues that go beyond just answering questions?" Amanda asked.

Jennifer spoke up. "Simple. Assign a young adult to each of our rooms. We'll station them just outside the door where they can sit with whoever is waiting, make sure no one enters the rooms if someone is already in with us. If we get someone who chooses to seek the Sacrament, our runners can get them over to Father Jorge."

"It sounds a little like an assembly line to me, but I'm not sure we have any other options. All this will take time to coordinate and set up. After the next talk, the teens will be in their small groups, so we can't change out the rooms until after that. What we need is an activity that keeps them occupied *and* keeps them out of the rooms while we set up. Any ideas?" Amanda continued.

"Trust walks are always a good time filler. That would get the teens out of the room, and since the next talk tonight is about trust, why not send them on a five-minute trust walk?" Jennifer suggested.

"Perfect!" Amanda stated, putting her hand up to receive a few high-fives. "They already have their colored headbands, so they can use those as blindfolds. The path that loops from here to the dining hall and then down by the basketball court should be a perfect distance. Some uphill walking, some down. Great idea!" Amanda smiled.

One of the things Brother Thomas had grown to appreciate about Amanda, was how easily she could surrender control in situations like these. He had worked with one other Youth Minister who wasn't as open about getting feedback or asking for suggestions. And, as was expected, that teen program had far less participation, both from the teens as well as adult and young adult volunteers. He hoped he would have the same trust in whatever groups he worked with during his ministry. He saw the value in allowing the Holy Spirit to move the program through whatever volunteers were available.

"Okay," Amanda stated, "It's not an ideal plan. But I guess we can make this work. Let's go with this new plan. Prayer Warriors unite!"

And with that, she placed her hand in the center of the group, palm facing down. Each of the others in the circle added their hand on top of hers.

"Form of a pillar of fire!" she said.

The rest took turns, choosing what shape their spiritual superpower would take for the night. Jennifer said she would be Living Water, and Stephen said his power would be the Voice of God. Brother Thomas took a moment, then, smiling, shared what was highest on his mind.

"I don't know if red vines are spiritual or not," he said, holding up a handful of the candy in his other hand, "but they should be. Shape of a flexible, bendable, twisty red licorice!" he said, loud enough to draw the attention of half of the room.

The other three paused a moment, then burst out laughing.

"Okay, let's get started," Amanda said, small tears of joy in her eyes.

Stephen stepped away first, raising his hand, shouting loudly, "God is good!"

Some of the teens responded, "All the time!"

Stephen continued, raising the volume, "And all the time!"

This time, more than half the room responded, echoing back a resounding, "God is good!"

Thomas felt a comfortable, inner warmth begin to rise. These little things the team did might seem silly to anyone outside of the retreat, but he knew this was what made youth ministry magic. He had already learned, if you wanted to connect with teens, you had to be a kid at heart. The more serious someone was, the less effective they would be. Brother Thomas had already witnessed this with a few adults, and even some young adults. They came into the program with a ton of desire but lacked the ability to drop their ego. Perhaps that was why he felt so at home with teens. They reminded him what it was like to be young. As he matured, taking on the responsibility of leading others in their spiritual journey, he hoped he would find joy in never growing old.

Having achieved the task of obtaining the attention of the teens, Stephen began to lead the room in song. Amanda pulled Thomas aside.

"You seem to have made a connection with Beth tonight. Are you okay if I put her as your runner?" she inquired.

"Sure. I like Beth. She's got a great rapport with the teens. I'd love to work with her."

"Then it's agreed," Amanda stated. "Time to get the group going for the next session. That gives us about an hour – call it an hour and a half – until adoration starts. Once the trust walk begins, can you set up the room for

Father Jorge? You'll have to do it right after the next small group session ends. Let's put him in the Mercy room. I'll have Jennifer set up the rooms you two will use. We can use the Hope and Faith rooms for you two."

Brother Thomas nodded in agreement.

"By the way, Amanda, I wanted to thank you for letting me work this retreat. It's been so much fun so far," he shared. "No problem, Thomas. It's been great seeing how much you've grown in the two years since you left for Steubenville," she told him.

They shared a quick hug, and then Amanda headed to the front of the room, singing along with everyone else. Thomas found a chair on the side of the room where he could watch the speaker, yet still keep his eyes on the faces of as many teens as possible. One by one, his precious red vines disappeared.

# CHAPTER ELEVEN
## ADORATION

A few hours later, Thomas glanced around the re-arranged room they would be using for the rest of the night. The classroom-style rows of chairs had been removed, replaced by a less formal arrangement. Gone, too, were the podium and video screen, replaced by a large table covered in a white sheet. On top of the table were set several candles, and a small vase, filled with wildflowers from the hills just outside the room. Amanda had also removed the snack table and had placed the water dispenser out of the way in a small alcove.

Outside the opened doors, Brother Thomas could hear the teens being led through their trust walks. The laughter that echoed through the still night air brought a smile to his face. As he was about to ask Amanda about the status of Father Jorge, the priest entered the room. Father Jorge was wearing a bright red chasuble, with a rainbow-striped stole that was decorated with images of cartoon characters. Father Jorge had obviously worked with teens before.

Thomas watched as Father Jorge walked to the far corner where Amanda and Jennifer were quietly reviewing the list of topics that Jennifer would need to bring to Amanda's attention, should any of the teens bring one of them up. Amanda paused her conversation, turning to give Father Jorge a huge hug. Unable to make out what the three were saying, Thomas turned his attention to the other side of the room where Stephen was leading the music team in one final rehearsal of the vocal harmonies, giving Brother Thomas chills. They had been blessed with such beautiful voices for this retreat.

Those few young adults who had not been assigned to a small group were waiting near the doors, trying their best to stay warm. Thomas knew it was good that the teens were outside right now, even though it was a bit cold. The laughter they shared and the cool night air would help them find a quiet space inside when they were asked to do so. It would also help keep them awake. Keeping teens awake for the late night session was always a challenge on retreats. Any conversations from here forward would be gently spoken, even whispered at times, and the lighting in the room would remain dim. A perfect environment for adoration, but also a perfect environment for sleep.

Still, creating this quiet environment was important. For it was here that God would reach these young people, speaking to them heart to heart. Thomas knew there was nothing that he or the leadership team had left to do. It was in God's hands now.

One by one, the small groups finished their trust walks, finding their way back to one of the doors leading into the large room. There, they were greeted as they arrived, and instructed to remove their blindfolds as they entered. Brother Thomas watched the faces of the teens as they moved slowly from bright smiles to quiet reverence. He could tell they had an understanding of what was about to take place. They crossed the threshold in silence, the memory of recent laughter gently fading away.

When the final teen was seated, Amanda spoke softly to the group, explaining the process for the night.

She gently explained the difference between going to reconciliation with Father Jorge and going to one of the advising rooms. Amanda then introduced Kevin and Kylie, explaining their role for the night, reminding the group that only a priest can perform the sacrament. Finally, she introduced Father Jorge.

Father Jorge stood, sharing a little about himself to help those gathered feel comfortable coming to him for reconciliation. He then asked the teens to bow their heads and take a moment to quiet their thoughts. He led them through an examination of conscience as the teens sat in silence. After a few minutes had passed, he gave Stephen a nod, and the music team began to play. Father Jorge, assisted by one of the young adults, lit the incense cone and votive candles. He then asked everyone to kneel, removing the white cloth covering the monstrance and exposing the Blessed Sacrament. They knelt in silent adoration as the music team played softly.

As the music faded once more, Father Jorge led the room in a few final prayers, then stood up, letting the teens know they could return to their chairs if they chose, though most remained kneeling. He invited those who were interested in seeking reconciliation to form a line along one wall. As he left the room, Jennifer motioned for Thomas to follow along, and the three stepped out into the cold night air. Father Jorge took the shorter path around the corner of the building, while Jennifer and Thomas turned the opposite way, heading in the direction of the rooms they had been assigned.

As they approached their rooms, Thomas began to feel a nervousness within. Try as he might, he couldn't settle his fears. His hands began to shake. This would be the first time he would be in an official ministry position, listening to the concerns of teens who were barely junior to him in age. He began to question if he was ready, if he would know what to say. And yet, he also knew there was no turning back now. He had made a commitment, and he was going to see it through. As if sensing his nervousness, Jennifer reached over and took his hand.

"You'll be fine, Brother Thomas. You've got this. Just have faith, and remember, you won't be speaking your words tonight, you're going to be speaking His."

Thomas forced a brave smile on his face, hoping she was right. Looking up, he saw Beth sitting in a chair outside one of the doors, wrapped tightly in a blanket.

"Hey, Brother Thomas! Looks like I'm stuck with you all night. I mean, glad to see you!"

Her attempt at humor was greatly appreciated, as it calmed some of his fear. She reached a hand out to him, holding a small, white rose.

"Not sure where this came from. I found it on my chair when I got here. Thought you might want to have it," Beth said with a knowing look in her eye.

"Thank you, Beth. Well, I did pray for a sign. Here I am entering a room they named *Faith*, and a white rose, the sign of purity, appears," Thomas shared, accepting the rose from Beth.

"You'll do great! Remember, if you need anything, I'll be right out here," she said, then continued, "Oh, yeah. In case you need them, I brought a stash."

Beth shifted her blanket slightly, revealing a full carton of red vines. Brother Thomas laughed softly. His reputation was already starting to spread.

"Oh my God," Thomas said, wincing slightly. He looked up to the sky and whispered, "Sorry big guy. That one slipped."

Thomas shook his head, entering the room he would be using for the next few hours. Inside he found two folding chairs set on either side of a small table. On the table was a tall, thin glass vase, a pillar candle, a Bible, and a box of Kleenex. He placed the rose in the vase, filling it with water from the bottle he had with him. He then lit the candle and walked towards one of the corners to gather his thoughts. He took a deep breath, softly raising his thoughts in prayer. Deep inside his heart, he knew there was a chance he could sit in this room all night without a single person coming to see him. Though a part of him truly wanted to participate in what he was about to do, he also told God he wouldn't be upset if he spent the entire time alone. At that moment, there was a knock at the door.

"Come in," he called, turning towards the door as it slowly opened.

As the door opened, Thomas recognized one of the teens he had been watching through the weekend. She had kept mostly to herself, especially at meal time, which had raised a few concerns. And, though she had participated in the activities throughout the day, he could tell she did so with reluctance. It was more than just timidity or shyness on her part. It was as if she was genuinely trying to blend into the background; as if she wanted to disappear. He stood to the side of the door, motioning her in. She took the chair closer to the door, and Thomas sat in the other.

"You're Theresa, right?" he asked.

The girl nodded, not looking directly at him.

Brother Thomas was about to speak when he remembered how Father Dominic would never speak first during their conversations. Although he didn't like it at the time, he had grown to understand the purpose behind the gesture. Father Dominic was letting him know that he was just as comfortable sitting in silence as he was in conversation. He wanted Thomas to make the decision to open up and share, versus coaxing him into speaking. In that moment, Brother Thomas decided to do the same with Theresa.

He knew it had already taken great courage to stand up in the large group room, to be the first to come see him. If he opened dialogue too soon, the part of her that was afraid of being seen might win the battle, causing her to shrink even further inside the safety she felt in her isolation. And so he let God do His work and waited patiently for her to open up first.

They sat there for what seemed an eternity, though Thomas knew that was a trick caused by the nervousness he felt. More likely, a minute or two had passed. Theresa sat unmoving, head down, chin almost touching her chest, staring intently at the floor. Her hair hung loosely on both sides of her head, creating a shield around her face. He couldn't see her expression, leaving him to wonder just how deep her pain might be. Just as he was about to speak first, he saw a small circle of darkness appear near her knee. A tear had fallen from her cheek. As if the sacrifice made by that small tear provided her the permission she needed to speak, her thoughts began to form into words.

"So, you're probably wondering why I'm here, huh?" she said, more of a statement than a question.

Brother Thomas waited patiently, silently.

"I mean, I already told just about everyone I didn't want to come on this stupid retreat in the first place. I'm here 'cause my mom made me. I don't care that much about all this religion stuff. Most of what we do just doesn't make sense to me," she blurted out, then paused, obviously trying to push her emotions back inside.

Brother Thomas continued being a silent witness. Theresa raised her head just enough to look at him, perhaps trying to gauge what he might be thinking about. As their eyes met, Thomas could feel the deep longing for answers inside her heart. He tried to give her a small smile, but it came out wrong, more like a grimace, as if he had just tasted something sour. She turned her gaze back to the floor. Her shoulders slowly rose perceptibly and then fell back again, a silent sigh escaping into the room. Brother Thomas began to wonder if he was prepared for what she might say next.

Finding strength somewhere inside, or perhaps finally giving up her fears, she continued, almost whispering.

"I know my name tag says Theresa, but that's just what the world calls me, I guess. My real name is The Endlessly Dying Girl. Nothing in my life makes any sense, which I guess is why I'm not a huge fan of religion since it's supposed to offer you all these answers and shit. But that's just not where I'm at, you know?"

Brother Thomas flinched slightly at her choice of words. It wasn't like he hadn't heard teens curse before. It was just that, once they knew they were with someone who was one day going to be a priest, most of the people he spoke with cleaned up their language quite a bit. The fact that she openly swore in front of him made the hairs on the back of his neck vibrate. He began measuring the silence as he waited. If he counted thirty or more seconds, he would have to say something, if even just to ask her to share more. As he counted, Theresa continued.

"Sorry about swearing. I guess I'm not supposed to in the presence of a holy person. That's what my mom tells me, anyway. Says that God hears every word we utter and that he will punish us if we don't behave right."

She looked up at him, pain and anger clearly evident in her eyes.

"But you should hear the words pour out of her mouth! If God was going to punish someone for swearing, I would think he would have started with her by now."

There was another pause as she fought back tears, blinking her eyes to spread the gathering moisture.

"But maybe he already did. Maybe that's why I'm the one always dying now. I don't know."

Brother Thomas prepared himself. This was the second time in the fairly short conversation that she had mentioned the word 'dying' in conjunction with herself. He began to grow anxious that there might be something behind these admissions. He opened his mouth to speak, but before words came forth, she went on.

"I just wish I really knew," she said, pausing a moment, continuing in a softer voice, "I just wish I knew he was really there. I mean, I pray to him like I'm supposed to. But some nights I just stare up into the sky, and I can't make myself believe there's anyone out there. I mean, what kind of God would create a universe this big, if all we have is this one little fucked up planet?"

Another pause.

"Sorry, there I go swearing again. I mean, how do we know, Brother Thomas? How do we really know?"

Thomas breathed deeply, holding her gaze.

"That's the great mystery of faith, Theresa. We can't prove it. Faith has to come from what we believe in our hearts, not what we know with our minds."

He knew she had probably heard all this before, but he had to start somewhere. He was still not quite sure where this conversation was heading. To find out, he would have to take a more active role. Suddenly, Theresa's expression changed, taking on a look of disappointment, or disbelief. She snorted softly, indicating the extent of her displeasure with his response.

"So, tell me this, why did you decide to be a priest then? What made you look at all the suffering in this world; children without parents, kids living on the streets, parents getting divorced, and think it was still worth fighting for? What do you see that I can't?" she begged.

Brother Thomas paused, considering the best words to say. Instead, he asked her a question.

"I think, before I respond, that I need to understand something about why you are asking. Twice already in our conversation, you mentioned dying. That you are always dying; or forever dying?" He paused, waiting for her to respond.

"Endlessly dying. Yeah, that's me. "

"Can you tell me what that means?" he inquired.

# CHAPTER TWELVE
## THE ENDLESSLY DYING GIRL

Theresa sat in silence for a long, long moment. She simply stared at Thomas with a slightly puzzled expression, as if she was trying to judge how interested he really was in what she had to say. Something about her mood and the way she picked at the polish on her nails gave Thomas a feeling that he already knew what she was about to share.

"Yeah, endlessly dying," she began, pausing for a moment longer as her thoughts fell into place. "It just kinda fits the way I feel inside most of the time."

Brother Thomas watched as her expression changed as the words came out. He could tell this was the first time she had found a way to express what she had been trying to understand for some time.

"I guess it's like this," she went on, slowly. "A few years ago, my school went on a trip to the Grand Canyon. It felt like we were on that bus forever. When we finally got to Arizona, we stopped at some stupid gift shop or something that said it sold authentic Native American jewelry. It was mostly crap, though. We were going to be there for an hour, you know, have lunch, stretch, all that, so I wandered off into the desert. I came across this little lake, not much bigger than a swimming pool, so lake probably isn't the right word. More like a pond, I guess?

"Anyway, near the edge of the water was this one little flower. It looked like it was struggling to stay alive. Like it was just close enough to the water to not die, but not close enough to live. As soon as I saw it, I realized, that's exactly how I feel. Like, I'm just hanging on, at the edge of the water, not really living, yet I know I'm not going to die, either. I'm just in limbo, I guess," she shrugged, shifting her position in the chair. "It's like I'm forever stuck in the middle of getting what I need to survive on one side, and the dying part on the other side. Like I can't choose which way to go."

Theresa looked up from whatever spot it was on the floor she had been staring at. Their eyes met, and Brother Thomas held her gaze. He tried to keep his expression peaceful, relaxed. He wanted her to know that he was not only interested in what she had to share but genuinely concerned as well. The gentle glow in his eyes encouraged her to continue her story.

"I mean, I want to live, don't get me wrong. I just don't seem to ever have the strength to move towards the water. The desert, which is my life, keeps me dying just enough that I can't do anything about my situation. Every time I think things are getting better, another part of me dies. I'm back to being stuck right where I was, trapped between two worlds; the one I live in, and the one I want to believe is real," she shared.

Theresa began to fidget with her fingernails, slowly peeling off the polish. It reminded Thomas of the habits he had during his periods of distress; like scratching at his face. Unconsciously, his hand went up, his fingers scratching at the two-day stubble on his cheek. It was just what happened, not something he could control. He knew it had to be the same for her.

"That's quite the analogy, Theresa. I can see that little flower caught between the desert and water. Tell me, have you always felt like this?"

One part of him didn't want her to answer, but he knew he had to. If he was going to help her, provide her the support she really needed, he had to know if something had happened. He had to know if she had been abused, or abandoned, or worse. He knew this was what she wanted from him, to take away her pain. Yet, he also knew, just like Father Dominic had left him to find his way through his own pain, Thomas would have to let her do the heavy lifting. It was better for him to show her how to find the answers she needed than to give them to her. As painful as it might be, he couldn't fix it. She had to.

"I guess it all started when my parents split up," she explained. "They really weren't all that happy being together, I guess. I mean, I tried to be a good kid, keep my brother and me from bothering them too much. I don't know, but I think they were probably happier before they had kids. I mean, why would two people get married and start a family if they weren't happy being with each other? They must have been happy when they got married. The pictures from their wedding make them look like they were. But I never knew that part of them. I only knew the ugly stuff, the fighting. And they fought all the time. Like, all the time.

"Most of the time, they tried to fight all quiet like. They'd go in their bedroom, leave my brother and me watching TV, and they'd start off all quiet," Theresa shook her head, glancing briefly at Brother Thomas. "But they weren't good at quiet. One would start getting loud, and you could hear the other one tell them to keep it down. Eventually, they would both be yelling. I guess they didn't think we could hear them, or that we weren't paying attention. Every time they started, my brother Anthony would come over and sit right beside me, sometimes in my lap. He's three years younger than me, so he was like six back then. He doesn't come to me that often anymore. Maybe he's learned how to deal with it on his own like I have."

Thomas could tell Theresa wasn't really 'dealing with it'. She was still very much troubled by the events of her youth, as she would be until she found a way to forgive her parents, and herself. He said a quick prayer that she would find this freedom soon.

"Anyway, the night it happened," Theresa continued, drawing Thomas' attention back to her words, "I was at the kitchen table doing homework, and Anthony was playing video games in the front room. Mom was in the kitchen cooking dinner. I could tell she was getting frustrated about something because when I asked for help with one of my math problems, she about bit my head off. That was when Dad came home and the fighting started. Only this time, they started right in the kitchen. They didn't try to be quiet about it or nothing. Just started right in. Mom yelled at Dad the minute he got in the door. I don't remember what it was, I was just hoping they wouldn't notice I was right there in the room with them. That's the first time I wanted to be invisible, you know, like a superhero. Endlessly Dying Girl, that's my superhero name. So far I've only found one power, being invisible. That was the night I found it.

"As they were fighting, Mom was cleaning some of the stuff in the sink. I guess that's what she does when she's angry. Dad said something, though I don't recall what exactly. I just remember Mom getting super pissed off. I could see it in her eyes. I knew something bad was going to happen, and I couldn't watch. I closed my eyes, just for a moment. I thought, maybe if I didn't see them, then I would really disappear. You know how little kids think. That's when I heard the crash. I opened my eyes to see what happened. My dad was kneeling on the ground. He was holding his face, and I could see blood between his fingers. I don't know what Mom threw at him, but she must have hit him hard enough to knock him over.

"I got up and ran to Anthony. That's when I realized I was invisible, 'cause I ran right between them and they didn't even look at me. I took one look at Dad. The look on his face was scary, like really scary. I grabbed my brother by the hand and we ran into my closet, shutting the door behind us. I pushed him to the back, behind the long dresses Mom kept in there, then I crawled in beside him. All I could hear was Dad grunting, Mom screaming, and stuff breaking. It was intense. I don't know how long it lasted. Eventually, the cops showed up. I guess the neighbor called. Mom got taken away in an ambulance. Dad was in the back of the police car. He never came back after that. Not even to pick up his stuff. Nice, right?" Theresa turned her head again to look at Brother Thomas., the pain and anguish she still felt were etched across her face.

Brother Thomas felt like she was telling his own story. His heart went out to Theresa. He knew what she was dealing with. Theresa sat there looking at him through the twin pools that filled her eyes, aching for his reply. Everything he had learned about dealing with situations like this hadn't even come close to preparing him for what to do. He struggled to find the right words, knowing he had to say something, anything that would help with what she was dealing with.

"By now," he began, "I'm sure you've been told that what happened wasn't your fault. That you didn't do anything wrong and that it has nothing to do with what type of daughter you were. I don't think you came here tonight to hear more of that. Although you may still be dealing with those questions, you asked a few others that tell me your true questions right now are much deeper. I think perhaps you may have already come to realize, even if you did accept that there was nothing you could have done to prevent what happened, these other questions would still be there. And it is these questions that are causing you the most pain.

"Now, I didn't know you back then. Heck, we just met yesterday, which means I can't say for sure that what I'm about to say is exactly what you're feeling, but I think it is. You see, I lived through a similar experience of my own, although I wasn't there to see what happened. I found out about it after. But, if what I say doesn't feel right, if you don't think I really get where you are coming from, stop me. I'm no expert, that's for sure, and I don't want you to feel like your emotions and your thoughts are not being heard. I want to hear you, I want to understand. And so I'm going to share with you what I believe is in your heart right now, is that okay with you?"

Thomas waited for her to reply, looking at her with soft eyes, trying to express his sincerity about his desire to help her find peace. He watched as the chaos of her emotions played out across the expressions of her face. At times, he could see her fear of trusting someone. Other times he could see the same despair he had felt years ago; the darkness that had challenged him to run away. Her mouth opened and closed several times, as if her words wanted to come out, but her mind feared the finality of speech. Finally, she nodded her head ever so slightly, while her knuckles turned bone white, her hands tightly gripping the corners of her chair.

He could not only see her fear, he could smell it, too. A misshapen form flashed in and out of visibility above her head, and the air had the smell of hot metal. The connection he felt went beyond anything he had sensed before. It wasn't like he could read her thoughts, but he could read her emotions, as clearly if they were his own. Something told him to give her a moment, to let the part of her that was tired of holding on to her pain gain some control. When the shape above her stopped flashing and became more solid, he began to speak. As he did, Thomas felt a strange presence in the room touching his heart and softening his voice. Each word he uttered came out like a dove, landing gently on her mind, calming her soul.

"During the first part of our conversation, you asked me a couple of questions: how do we know God is really there, that He is listening to us; and you asked me why I decided to become a priest." He paused. "I think both of these questions tie into your story about being the Endlessly Dying Girl and your power to disappear. I have to tell you, I have seen you practicing this weekend; the way you sit alone at meals, or trying not to be too involved in the activities with your small group. Everything you do seems to be just enough so no one thinks something is wrong. You have a powerful way of going unnoticed.

"Now, I feel like you want to believe you have a purpose, that there is some reason you are here, and that there is more to life than what you've experienced so far." He paused, hoping she would look at him as he spoke. When she didn't move, he went on. "Because of what happened between your parents that night, you took on a great deal of your mother's pain. Not physically, but spiritually. In some way, you felt like that was you in the kitchen, and you want to believe you would have stood up to your dad, that you would have defended yourself. A part of you is angry with your mom for not being as strong as you would have wanted yourself to be in that moment. I think, that night, you lost hope."

Theresa nodded slightly.

"And, you lost your purpose. You thought your purpose was to become a woman like your mom. She was your role model. She was the one you looked up to most. She was the one person who had always been there for you. But you don't see her like that anymore. She's not your rock; she's not your strength.

"And your dad, the one person in your life who isn't supposed to hurt you, or anyone else, he took all that from you. And then he left, moved away, disappeared," Brother Thomas said, once more pausing as he could feel her emotions begin to overload. "In fact, you lost quite a bit that night, which is why you feel like you're so empty inside, why it's so easy for you to disappear. No one has come and taken the place to guide you; you haven't found your beacon of hope."

Theresa had begun choking back tears.

"That part of you that was lost, that innocence of childhood that you had to sacrifice so you could take care of your brother, that's the half of the flower that's in the desert. That's where your hope and your faith are struggling to hold on. The other half of the flower still clings to the belief that your life has to have meaning."

Theresa raised her head to look at him. Her expression was tight, every muscle in her face struggling to not let go. She was carrying so much, too much. Thomas sighed deeply. He would have to gauge his next words carefully. Theresa was in such a vulnerable and delicate state, if he said too much, he could lose her once more.

"Right now, every time you choose to use your power, to disappear, you feel like your mom that night. Helpless, frightened, and alone. The desert side is winning. You don't want to feel like this. But you don't know another way to feel."

He paused as she turned her face away, not wanting him to see her cry.

"I think you want that beacon of hope to be God, but you still have questions. Like, if He loved you as much as your Sunday School teachers said He does, then He would have stopped all this from happening, right? Why would He take away all that you had put your trust in? Why would He let your family fall apart? Part of you wants Him to respond. You want to ask Him why, and you want to tell Him how angry you are with Him for letting this happen."

As he had shared these final thoughts, the shape above her head began to swirl and toss, a symbol of her emotional storm boiling over. Suddenly, the shape froze as her emotions became calm and relaxed. A part of her began to understand and accept why she felt the way she did. She understood her anger at losing everything she believed in, and as she did, that calm quickly faded. Thomas could feel a dark heat rise within her, fueled by her burning pain. He watched as her emotional symbol changed into a dark, smoldering cloud that flashed and bristled with electric light.

Suddenly, as if he was watching a movie, Thomas saw images flash by, each one connected to a part of her anger. He saw her anger with her mom for not being strong enough to stand up for herself. He saw her anger at her father for not being patient enough to control himself. He saw her anger with God for not doing anything to take away her pain. He saw her anger at her brother for turning to her for support when she had no one to turn to herself. He saw how much it hurt her to be the one who had to be strong when she was desperately in need. He saw her grief as she was forced to move from the house she had been born in, and then from one apartment to another while her mom tried to make things work. He saw her visiting with her dad, being forced to have a chaperone with them. He felt her anger that she couldn't spend time with him without someone watching every move he made. He could tell that nothing about her life made sense after that night. Everything she felt, Thomas could somehow see, as if he had experienced it, too.

Inside her heart, he watched as Theresa finally let go. The pain she had been holding onto for so long gave way, and she burst into tears. Theresa buried her face in her hands, bent as low as she could in the chair, and let it out. As she cried, Brother Thomas said nothing. He knew he had to let this process take its own course. As painful as it was to watch, she had to go through this.

Eventually, there were no tears left. Her river of emotions was dry, but she was at peace. The storm had passed. She had survived. Thomas could see a spark flicker to life in the depths of her heart. Theresa had found something to take the place of her fear. She had found strength. He had witnessed both the death of her suffering and the birth of new hope.

Theresa's eyes were darkened from the stains left when mascara mixes with tears. Thomas handed her the Kleenex, remaining silent as she wiped away the mess. Between wipes, her chest heaved as she regained her composure. She looked at Brother Thomas for a moment, a shy smile on her face letting him know she would be okay.

Thomas had heard once that darkness was only the absence of light. Perhaps despair, then, was just the absence of joy.

In that moment, they had connected in ways neither of them had known before. Similar to his relationship with Father Dominic, Thomas knew he would be the one to help her find her way home. Though he would have to let her set the course, he would show up from time to time and help get her back on course. Somehow he knew that Theresa would be a part of his life for a long, long time.

"I know when I cried like that, when I finally let go of all of my anger, my frustrations, my fears, and doubts, it felt wonderful; as if I could fly. How do you feel right now?" Brother Thomas asked.

"I'm not sure yet," Theresa admitted, "I mean, I feel different inside, that's for sure. But, will it last?"

Smiling at her, he said, "Only for as long as you want it to. The choice is yours. I have a favor I want to ask, but I think I should answer your second question first. You wanted to know why I am learning to be a priest. I can only tell you this – I don't know why."

Theresa's expression changed to one of surprise.

"You see, I'm a lot like you, Theresa. I have the same questions about God, and even the same doubts, the same fears. In some ways, I have felt like I've been endlessly dying, too. I've been carrying around such a desperate desire to see Christ, to truly see him, not just in the actions of others, or in helping those in need, but to truly see him, as plain as I see you now," he admitted.

He could tell his admission shocked her as if she was unable to see someone living a religious life as ever having doubts about faith. And, to be honest, there were times he felt the same way.

"I think that's why I chose the priesthood as my career. I couldn't see any other position in life that would give me the answers I so desperately need. We may never understand why God asked you to endure the weight of your burden, and I don't think that weight has been fully lifted yet. All we can do is trust that there is a reason, there is a purpose. We can only hope that there will be a day in the future where you will find that what God gave you wasn't pain and suffering, but strength. One day you'll understand that if you hadn't gone through what you did five years ago, you would never be ready to face whatever God has planned for you next.

"I don't know if you have gone to Reconciliation in the past, maybe as part of your First Communion preparation, but I think you should go tonight. Father Jorge can help you so much more than I can. You can ask God to forgive you for carrying that much pain for so long, for being angry with your mom and dad, for being frustrated with your little brother for needing your support. You can also ask him to forgive you for doubting he was there, watching over you, protecting you, strengthening you even though you didn't know it. It's your choice, but I can honestly say that I think it will really help. Does that sound okay?"

Theresa nodded. He could tell she wasn't sure how much it would help, but she trusted him, and that was all he could ask for right now.

"When you speak to Father Jorge, remember, forgiveness isn't about saying that what happened was okay, and it's not about letting the people in your life off the hook for hurting you. It's about saying you are no longer going to let what they did affect you. It's about giving yourself the right to let go, to heal."

Theresa smiled at that thought, and he could sense that some of her burdens lifted even more in that moment. He stood up, took the wet Kleenex from her hands and helped her to her feet. She stood there for a moment, as if unsure what to do, then wrapped her arms around his neck, giving him the biggest hug she possibly could. He could tell she had given herself permission to feel loved, and so he let his love for her, for her situation, and for her trust in him pour into his return hug. Slowly, she let go, raising her head to look up at him with eyes that no longer looked distant and empty.

"Thank you," she whispered.

He saw that she wanted to say more, but couldn't find the words. In her eyes, he saw a vision. The little flower she had been, caught between life and death, no longer struggled. It stood strong, vibrant and powerful.

"I think I found my next superpower," she whispered as he led her to the door.

"Really?" he asked. "And what might that be?"

"What...and spoil the surprise?" she giggled, turning to walk back outside.

Brother Thomas chuckled in appreciation of her new found joy. The sound echoing deep within his heart.

# CHAPTER THIRTEEN
## BE THOU MY VISION

Brother Thomas followed Theresa out into the cold night air. He glanced down at Beth, wrapped tightly in her blanket, sitting just a few feet away.

"Beth, I need a favor from you please," Thomas asked quietly.

Beth looked at Theresa for a moment. She slowly turned her head to face Brother Thomas, a look of concern on her face.

"Theresa would like to seek Reconciliation now," Brother Thomas told her. "Can you walk her over and make sure she gets in the front of the line?"

"Of course!" Beth exclaimed, nearly jumping out of her chair.

Beth took Theresa by the hand, pulling her close and wrapping her tightly in the blanket with her.

"Thanks, Beth. You're the best," he said.

He watched as the two girls, arms looped around each other's shoulders, began to disappear into the night. He could hear them whispering to each other, but couldn't make out what they said.

"Oh, Beth, I almost forgot," he called out, watching as they stopped, slowly turning his way.

"Stay with this one, okay?" he instructed.

Beth gave him a mock salute, saying, "Yes, sir! Shall I send over the next victim?"

Brother Thomas chuckled. He was about to say 'yes', then changed his mind.

"Not quite yet. I'll put a candle in the window when I'm ready. Could you let Amanda know?"

"Your wish shall be granted, El Padre Porvenir!"

And then, the pair was gone, lost in the gathering mist. He stood in the doorway for a moment, listening to their quiet laughter, until that, too, faded away. Thomas turned and went back inside, suddenly aware of how incredibly cold it was. Closing the door, he surveyed the room, then dropped to his knees to pray.

"Father, I trust you are there. I want to thank you for bringing Theresa to me tonight. It's been some time since I've felt like I've connected with someone that deep. I know I am on the path to help others, to make a difference in the lives of those suffering, and I am so grateful that you have chosen to use me in this way tonight. And yet, so frustrated that still inside of me, even with all that I witness, there still lingers doubts. Doubt about my faith, about being a priest, about all that I once believed so passionately. Where is that fire that used to consume me? Where is that passion that drove me to spend quiet hours at night praying, waking up early to meditate? It was such a powerful feeling once. I wish I knew where it went.

"These young people I am ministering to have so much more life inside than I ever remember having at this age. Some of them are already blessed with a faith that seems so far beyond what I've been able to find. They are the ones who should be wearing this tunic, not me. They are the ones who should be living these vows, not me."

Thomas paused, tilting his head up.

"Why have you chosen someone with such strong doubts as a part of your ministry? Why would you ask someone who struggles daily to accept your call to represent you, especially to these young people? I know I don't let it show on the outside, but these kids can tell. I know they can tell. They see what's really inside my heart, they feel my doubts. And I worry my doubts might make them doubt their faith, too."

Thomas hung his head once more. The burden of his doubts weighing heavily on his mind.

"God, I don't understand what it is that you are asking of me, why it is that you called to me so loud four years ago. Now, when I feel like I need you the most, to know you're there, you are strangely quiet, and I can't release these doubts in my heart."

His knees began to hurt from the hard floor, but Thomas didn't move.

"Maybe this is just part of my learning process. Perhaps, like Theresa was able to do tonight, I'll find whatever it is that I need to release, let it go, and once more become who you already see me as. I just don't see it in myself right now, and for that I'm sorry."

Brother Thomas spent a moment in silence, listening for any indication that God heard him, hoping for even the smallest response. When none came, he got back up, put the candle in the window, and sat back down, waiting to see who God might bring to him next.

Over the course of the next few hours, he met with several other teens. Some who had simple questions, some who were carrying burdens they couldn't identify, though none as deep as Theresa's. He thought of her throughout the evening between his other conversations, wondering how she was. He knew she hadn't completely overcome her struggle yet, that there was still a long way to go. But he also knew that she was young, she had time. Whatever small assistance he had provided tonight, she would have to walk the rest of the way on her own. He had faith she would make it. She seemed stronger than he had been when he carried a burden similar to hers. He saw an inner strength in her that he didn't see in many teens. Deep as her pain was, it never fully defeated her. She always remained one step above despair, and that took strength. She obviously had a large part in God's plan, and he hoped he would someday hear the rest of her story, the part where she found the blessing buried deep beneath the pain.

Eventually, one of the young adults came to let him know there were no more teens waiting to see Father Jorge. He walked back to the large group room, his thoughts lost in another world. Upon entering the room, he caught a glimpse of Theresa, sprawled out on the floor, fast asleep. He smiled. She probably hadn't slept that deeply and that peacefully for a long, long time. Beth was beside her, holding Theresa's head in her lap, gently stroking her long, black hair. He smiled at Beth as their eyes met, and she smiled back. Beth looked tired, her eyes reflecting that somewhat empty, yet peaceful look of someone who had recently cried. Like the feeling one has walking outdoors just after a storm, sensing both the quiet of the present moment, along with the residue of the tempest lingering in the air.

He didn't know that much about Beth, other than what they had shared earlier at dinner, but he could tell she carried the same strength he had seen in Theresa. There was a way teens and young adults carried childhood scars that Brother Thomas could see; as if they were tattooed on their souls. They had a lost, longing, yet hopeful look about them, and a deep sense of wisdom far beyond their years. Though harder to reach, he knew if he could break through, he would find tremendous strength.

Thomas wished he could take away their pain and struggles of being young. But that was part of what made them who they were meant to be. He knew he couldn't cut them from their chrysalis. They had to struggle to find their own way out, even if it took every ounce of strength they had. Otherwise, they might never become whole.

As the music team reached the end of the song they were performing, Father Jorge let the silence linger. He had taken a position in front of the Blessed Sacrament, kneeling in honor to the miracles he had witnessed tonight. After a moment, he stood and addressed the room.

"Tonight has been a tremendous blessing, especially for those who have reconciled their sins. I ask you all to remember how you felt tonight, to recall how powerful it was to let go of those burdens. And know that this is how Christ wants us to feel, not just in special moments, but in every moment. This is the peace that he has for us, and all we need to do is accept it. And so, tonight, let as raise our voices together, in unity and in strength. Let us pray…"

As Father Jorge led the teens in the final prayers, Brother Thomas glanced over at where Beth and Theresa were now kneeling. Once more he saw them with arms around each other's shoulders. Beth's blanket was draped across their shoulders and necks, reminding Thomas of a superhero cape. He had a vision of the two women, dressed in full costume, fighting side by side to help free young people like themselves from the hardships of life.

The vision vanished as Father Jorge brought the prayers to a close, draping the monstrance once more with the cloth. Amanda walked to the front of the room, gave the teens a few, final instructions, and then sent them to their cabins for the night. Brother Thomas watched as they slowly filed out, some staying behind as an impromptu jam session formed with members of the music team. Some of the other teens continued the deep conversations they had been quietly whispering during Adoration, and in one corner, a group of teens and young adults were praying over some of their peers.

Thomas could feel the profound sense of relief that had developed over the past few hours, as one teen after another had experienced the benefits of Reconciliation. He breathed in deeply, praying that some of the newly born hope would penetrate his heart as well. He knew he was long overdue for a rebirth of Spirit in his own life. Perhaps some of what these teens had found would find refuge within his life as well.

Amanda broke through his thoughts, calling him over to debrief with the team. After their fairly short conversation, with a round of thanks being passed along to all for their participation in the evening's events, Amanda dismissed the team, reminding them morning prayers would come early, sharing her hope that they would each find the rest they so well deserved.

Brother Thomas walked outside, heading back to his room. He knew the few hours left for sleep tonight would be barely enough for him to recover from this weekend. But, he was still young. He would recover. Luckily, he had a non-stop flight back to Pittsburgh, and a half-hour Uber ride from the airport back to school. He could catch a few hours of sleep then.

As he walked the path to his cabin, his thoughts were distracted by a sudden brightening. Thomas paused his stride, looking up to see the full moon sneaking through a small opening in the clouds. He stood gazing into the heavens, suddenly present to the wonder of God's creation all around him. The evening mist whispered past like small tufts of cotton, pulled and stretched until they were transparent. Above him, the clouds continued to pull aside, letting more light from the moon seep through, exposing the dark shadows of the redwoods against the star-filled sky.

He was envious of those trees and how far they extended above where he stood, reaching closer to the beauty of the sky than he ever could. Beyond those tree tops, even further distant still, the clouds continued to part. It reminded him of a curtain drawing open, a performance about to begin. The light from the moon increased as the stage of the sky came to life. It drew Brother Thomas in, offering him comfort, escape.

Thousands of stars winked back at him, their majesty pushing his thoughts down new paths. How many stars were there? How far did their light travel to meet him here? Did they shine because he could see them? And beyond the stars, what was hidden there? Was this where he would find God, out beyond the furthest star? Perhaps this is why he felt so distant to God, so far away.

As if on cue, the stars seemed to flow towards him, thousands upon thousands of stars moving in unison. He felt transfixed by their beauty. It was as if the entire heavens had heard his request to be closer to God, and, since he couldn't approach the stars, they now approached him. His knees began to buckle, and his head grew faint. Within his heart, the deep longing he had felt for so long pulled at him to fly out and meet the stars. He looked down to his feet, certain he would see the earth below disappearing forever as he leaped forward to live among the angels. But his feet were still firm on the concrete path. He glanced back up, praying the vision hadn't left.

As the stars continued to grow larger, more luminous and more brilliant in each moment, Thomas began to sing. Softly at first, the words poured forth, the sound emanating from deep within his core.

> *Be Thou my vision, O Lord of my heart;*
> *Naught be all else to me, save that Thou art;*
> *Thou my best thought, by day or by night;*
> *Waking or sleeping, Thy presence my light.*

Thomas jumped as, halfway through, a second voice joined in, and then a third. Turning towards the sound, he saw two of the vocalists from the music team on the path above him. They stood like Thomas did, eyes cast upwards, watching the sky. Were they witnessing the brilliance of the same celestial dance? Or was this vision only in his own mind? Looking back to the heavens, he saw the stars had once more returned to their homes, the radiant splendor was gone, though the moon still shone, full and bright, a soft halo surrounding the heavenly orb.

"Wow," Vicky softly voiced, picking back up where the song had left off.

> *Be Thou my wisdom, and Thou my true word;*
> *I ever with Thee, and Thou with me, Lord;*

Brother Thomas and Danielle joined in.

> *Thou my great Father; thine own may I be;*
> *Thou in me dwelling and I one with Thee.*

They held the final note in perfect three-part harmony, the sound echoing softly in the surrounding woods. Eventually, the curtain of clouds drifted together, the evening mist turned to fog, and the most magnificent performance was complete.

Vicky was the first to move, clapping her hands and shouting, "Again! Again! Again!" like a three-year-old child.

Danielle turned to her, rolling her eyes. "Vicky, you're such a spaz."

Brother Thomas wiped at a trail of wetness on his cheek, not realizing his eyes had released tears. He glanced at the two young women who had shared this moment with him, wondering if they felt the same inner warmth that he did. He wanted to ask them a question, but they had already started to walk away. Danielle stopped a moment later and turned back.

"That was amazing, Brother Thomas. What an awesome God! Have a good night!"

Brother Thomas waved to the girls, watching them disappear around a corner of the path. He remained motionless for a moment more, wondering if he truly would find the sleep he so desired this evening. He could feel a powerful energy flowing through his veins as if his very blood was on fire. Thomas turned his head skyward, hoping for one last glimpse of the miraculous display. For a fleeting moment he saw the moon peek through the clouds, and then, it was gone. He shivered. The temperature outside his body was winning the battle against the warmth he felt within. Reluctantly, his feet began to carry him up the hill to his room, his mind was stirring with thoughts, his heart at peace.

As he went through the process of getting ready for bed, he wondered what his life would look like if he never became Father Thomas. He wondered what it would mean for his future if he continued as Brother Thomas, or simply went back to being just Tom. He wondered if he would continue in ministry, or if he would be called to do something else. As he lay his head on his pillow, he reached to the nightstand by his bed and retrieved his rosary beads, making it into the second decade, drifting in and out of slumber until the gradual approach of sleep became too heavy for his conscious mind to hold. Thomas drifted peacefully to sleep.

# CHAPTER FOURTEEN
## THE LITTLE FLOWER

That night he dreamed he was walking a narrow path through an endless garden of roses. Although it was night, the sky was ablaze with millions of stars shining together as bright as the morning sun. At some points on the path, the flowers bloomed abundantly. At other points, the flowers were sparse, almost non-existent, and sometimes there was nothing but bare stems. He wondered who took care of this garden, and why they didn't tend to the plants equally in all areas.

He also passed several statues standing watch on each side of the path. He paid little attention to these, as his mind was focused primarily on the road ahead, unsure where he might be going. As he peered into the distance, he saw nothing but the same garden as far as he could see, some sections rich with blooms, others sparse. He sensed a sweet stillness in the air around him.

"Hello, Thomas," a gentle voice called out, breaking the silence.

Startled, Thomas jumped to the side, turning to face the direction the voice came from. There on the path next to him was a woman dressed in the habit of the Carmelite nuns. With her face turned towards the ground, Thomas was unable to see who she was, and yet sensed a familiarity about her.

"Sorry I jumped," Thomas said, bashfully, his cheeks growing pink. "I will admit, I honestly thought I was alone out here."

"We're never really alone in life, are we?" she inquired. "God's always nearby. If you know where and how to look."

She giggled gently, still not raising her head.

Brother Thomas considered her words. He wished he could believe them without doubt. He knew he wanted to believe.

"Come, let's continue walking," she suggested, offering her hand for him to hold.

Brother Thomas placed his much larger hand around hers, turning his attention back to the path. They walked together in silence for a time, their footsteps on the gravel the only sound. Eventually, Thomas felt a bit embarrassed.

"I'm so sorry, Sister. You obviously know my name, but I was remiss in my politeness. I failed to ask you for yours. Might I do so now?"

"You may, but I believe we have already met. Do you not remember?" she asked.

Brother Thomas paused for a moment, stopping to turn towards his companion. Slowly, she raised her eyes from the path, allowing him to see her face. She held a timid, shy smile, and there was a faint blushing on her cheeks. Thomas searched his memory, wondering if he had known her as a child before she entered the convent. Or perhaps she was one of the nuns who visited his school every summer to recruit volunteers for one of the many missions overseas. Try as he might, nothing came to mind. She saw the look of struggle on his face and chuckled gently at his plight.

"No, we never met in person. But we did meet. Last year, at school. You wrote a paper about me. Well, about my life," she stated.

He thought back to his freshman year, seeking even the smallest slice of memory that would provide him with her name. And suddenly, it was clear. As recognition spread across his face, he heard her giggle, the sound like a thousand wind chimes in a warm spring rain.

"Ah, Thérèse," he beamed as he welcomed her. "Or should I say, Saint Thérèse of Lisieux."

He tried to use a French accent, but it came out sounding strange. She giggled, blushing even more.

He continued, "My final paper during my first year in college was about your life, short that it was, and how deeply your life has touched so many."

"Trust me," she said, "yours will touch more. Come, we still have quite a ways to walk." She gave his hand a slight tug, pulling him along.

Thomas was taken aback. What did she know about his future, and how much might she be willing to share? Holding her tiny hand in his, he stated, "I do not know what you may already be aware of, but I hope anything I might or might not do with my life will affect others for the good, and not for the bad."

Saint Thérèse held his gaze. She took a deep breath, then let it out in a sigh.

"Oh, Thomas. You are just like your namesake in the Gospel. You want to believe your future will be blessed, that you will set aside your doubts and move forward with ease through the rest of your life. Yet, remember, 'Blessed are those who have not seen and yet have believed,'" she said, sighing once more.

He knew those last words by heart. They were the words Jesus spoke to the Disciple Thomas, the evening he appeared after the Resurrection. He spoke them just before instructing his disciple to put his fingers in the nail holes in his hands, to touch his side where the spear had pierced him. Brother Thomas suddenly felt ashamed. It was true. He had such little faith. Why God was calling him to be a priest, he had no idea.

"You mustn't fret. God knows why he called you to walk this path. You may not understand, but you will. In fact, that's part of the reason why I'm here, Thomas," Saint Thérèse replied.

Thomas realized with regret that she could read his thoughts. He stifled his thoughts quickly. Here he was in the presence of one of the great Saints of the Church, and all he could think about was his own doubts and fears. Didn't this represent the answer he had been searching for? Wasn't this enough to allow him to let go of at least some of his doubt? Would he feel any different if Jesus himself stood here in front of him?

He noticed they had walked long enough for another statue to appear. Yet, unlike the previous statues he had passed, which were on either the left or right side of the path, this one stood in the middle. He could see the statue was of a young woman, her gaze cast downward, looking neither left nor right. He also noticed the flowers on the sides of the path here were different.

On one side, the blossoms were abundant, glorious. On the other, not a single flower was in bloom. Not even an unopened bud sat among the thorns. Curious, he turned to Saint Thérèse, wondering why this statue and this section of the garden were different.

"Have you not yet made the connection between the flowers and the statues? Take a moment and look back along the path as far as you can see. Tell me what you find there," she instructed, pointing her arm back the way they had just come.

As he looked back, he did notice a pattern. When the statue stood on the right side of the path, facing left, the path was abundant with blossoms on both sides. When it stood on the left side, facing right, the bushes were barren. Realizing the statues held the clue to this garden, he let go of her hand and walked slowly to the closest statue behind them. This one stood on the right side, and the flowers on both sides of the path here flourished.

He saw no thread or cable connecting the statue to the flowers. Examining the statue itself furthered no additional information. It appeared to be made out of a standard marble, and there were no symbols or carvings of any kind. He tried to move the statue, thinking that perhaps if he placed it on the other side, the flowers would cease to bloom. But it was far too heavy to budge. Then he looked into the statue's eyes.

Brother Thomas smiled. The statue was of his mentor and long-time friend, Father Dominic. He always found his mood lifted during their visits and considered that perhaps the happiness he had felt during this part of his life is what caused the flowers to bloom more abundantly. Or perhaps because Father Dominic was a good person, his presence was what helped the garden thrive.

Thomas continued on to the next statue, this one again on the right side. As he approached, he saw a definite diminishing of flowers. Not to the point of being barren, but definitely not as radiant as the last. Wondering who this new statue represented, he was filled with dismay as he gazed into its eyes only to find that it, too, bore the resemblance of Father Dominic. Were all the statues of the same man? Hurrying now, Thomas jogged to the next statue along the path, this one on the left side, the branches here completely bare. Looking into the eyes of this statue, he recognized the image of his father. If the statue of Father Dominic demonstrated a person of good values or character, and therefore those sections were blessed with glorious blossoms, then was his father the opposite? True, they hadn't had the best relationship over the years, especially since that dreaded event more than four years ago.

He continued heading back down the path to the next statue, once more among a barren section of the garden. Here he found the face of Robert, his first roommate from his freshman year. Brother Thomas stopped in his tracks. There was no way his relationship with Robert had been negative. And Robert had been one of the most generous and caring individuals he had ever known. In fact, Thomas had been devastated when Robert had been killed in a motorcycle crash, just days before their first year had ended.

Suddenly, a thought struck him, hard enough to make his heart skip a beat. These monuments did not represent an individual person, but a moment in time. They were part of his past, a part in which each of these individuals had played a significant role.

When Robert died from the motorcycle accident, that period of Thomas' life had been very deep and sorrowful. The depth of that sadness was very much represented by the complete lack of flowers and color of any kind. Here, in this section, the rose bushes were not only bare, but the thorns appeared larger. What stems and branches there were had been covered with a gray dust, the color of ash after a fire. He thought about how deeply his heart had burned with sadness at the loss of his friend. This section of the garden could not have more accurately represented what he had felt during that loss.

Looking back to the statue of his father, he realized that it reflected a recent period of sadness as well. Only two months after Robert had passed, Brother Thomas had found himself at another funeral. This time, for his dad. His relationship with his father had been fairly non-existent by then. They only spoke at holidays and occasional moments during the year.

For the first year after his father had disappeared, they had heard nothing from him. Not a call, not a letter. Nothing. It wasn't until Thomas graduated from high school that his father had finally reached out. Even then, their contacts held none of the usual expression of feelings that a traditional father and son relationship should have. In some ways, Thomas had already said goodbye to his father long before he died. Because of this, he had been more prepared to cope with the sorrow that had followed. Now, it wasn't hard to see the structure of this garden.

A few months after his father died, Brother Thomas had an experience of tremendous joy. Father Dominic had returned from an extended mission trip that had prevented the two from seeing each other for over a year. This section held an abundance of roses. The next major emotional moment of his life had happened just three months ago when Father Dominic had been assigned to be his Spiritual Advisor, and the flowers here were even more beautiful. With a smile, Brother Thomas walked to where Saint Thérèse stood. Their eyes locked together, each smiling at the other in gentle appreciation of the moment they shared. Saint Thérèse spoke first.

"So, do you think you have solved the riddle? Do you now understand the mystery of this garden that we are in?"

"I think so. I believe this garden represents my life. At least some key moments. These were times when I felt genuine bliss, or when my heart was broken. When the moment was one of sadness, the garden is barren, and the statue is on the left side. When the moment was one of joy, the garden is in full bloom, and the statue is on the right."

Thomas paused. Caught momentarily by the new statue that was standing in the middle of the path. Gazing into the eyes, he found this one was of Theresa, the End-lessly Dying Girl he had met earlier.

"I still don't understand why this statue is in the middle of the path..." his voice trailed off. "Perhaps this moment is one that shows the balance in life? Does it represent a time when both sadness and joy were in unison? Maybe this is a moment that is neither, and yet both?" he inquired, his face a witness to the depth of his thoughts.

Saint Thérèse sighed. He felt like he was back in grade school when his teacher tried to help him understand how to subtract fractions.

"To be true, all moments in life are balanced. There is both joy and pain in everything," she admitted. "Look at my life and you will see. There was tremendous struggle, points in which I cried out in my despair. And yet, I never lost the love I held for the infant Jesus, or for his Blessed Mother, the one who smiled at me so sweetly at a time when I, too, felt all was lost."

She was right. Even in the moments of his despair, Thomas still felt some sense of joy. He knew his dad had carried deep emotional pain from a life lived mostly in regret. His passing carried with it a hidden message, one telling of a soul trapped for years that could finally be set free. He knew his father had sought redemption shortly before passing, and he had tried to make amends with each of his children. The tears that filled those moments carried with them the cleansing joy of forgiveness. If emotions of relief, forgiveness, and joy permeated throughout those of sorrow, why was the garden devoid of any blooms at all?

And, likewise, the moments of joy also held great trepidation and concern. Brother Thomas struggled to capture his thoughts as his mind raced faster and faster, trying to solve the garden's riddle. He turned once more to the statue of Theresa, reviewing the events of their conversation, looking for a clue as to which way the statue should face. He knew she had walked into their meeting with much more sadness than she had at the end. And though he had sensed some relief as she let go of the pain she held inside, he knew that relief was temporary, at least for now. She had far more work to complete before she would be totally free of her past.

Those last few words echoed back to him.

*"…totally free of her past…"*

The words played over and over again in his mind. Why were they so significant? His thoughts turned back to his own past, the path through the garden.

*His own past!*

Was he meant to free himself of his past? If those moments were balanced, holding both happiness and sadness, then why wasn't that displayed? Every step he took, regardless of how many blossoms, or on what side of the path the statue was erected, it was his feet only that walked upon the path.

The fact that Theresa's statue was in the middle, was not because this memory held balance where others did not. Every moment in his past had once held the same. At some point, each moment had been chosen, become locked in place, no longer free. Once, the statues of his past had stood in the middle of the path he now walked, as the statue of Theresa did now. And, just as he would need to move Theresa's statue to continue walking this path, the earlier statues must also have been moved.

Thomas knew the only one who had walked every step of this path was standing in the shoes he was staring at, the ones covering his own feet. If anyone had chosen which side of the path the statues should be standing on, it had to be him.

Feeling somewhat faint, Brother Thomas looked back to Saint Thérèse for help. Reaching out, she grasped his free hand. Holding his hands in hers, she turned him to stand right before her, letting go only momentarily of his right hand to lay her palm against his cheek. It was the same gesture his grandmother had used to comfort him when he was a boy. He wondered how she knew.

"You're almost there. I can only help you a little more. The sun is rising in your world, and the time we have left in your dream is running low. This much I can say. The statues of your past arrived on the path the same as this one here."

She paused for a moment, motioning to indicate the statue of Theresa.

"At first, they looked neither left nor right. How do you think they turned to face the way they do? If these are your memories, and you chose to carry them with you, then who do you think chose the way these moments would be remembered?"

Suddenly, Thomas saw the connection, nodding gently as understanding overcame his mind.

"I did. I turned them. I chose to see each moment as being either a painful part or a joyful part of my past. For the death of my father, I chose sadness because of the relationship we were never able to develop. I chose it because I felt I had to. Because it was what most people in that situation would do. I felt too guilty to admit that, in a way, I was somehow glad he was gone. I was too ashamed to feel like I just wanted to get on with my life. So I took on the role of the grieving child, the role I thought the world expected me to play. I am the one that chose which side he should stand, which way he should turn."

Saint Thérèse smiled broadly. She pinched his cheek, hard enough to leave a red mark, then turned to the statue in front of them, gently pulling him to join her.

"Yes, Thomas. Yes," she whispered. "And the same holds true in every moment. Every part of your past, all of the choices were made by you. You and you alone held the power to mark these milestones in your life. Your time with Theresa tonight was of enough importance to become a new milestone.

"In fact, it was I who sent her to you. Well, I gave her a nudge, anyway. Just strong enough to push her to speak to you. She's a lot like I was. So frail and timid, full of so much despair and pain. So many feelings of loss, yet still so full of love for God. Her faith will go far, now that you have helped replant it in the fertile soil.

"You see, Thomas, Theresa represents the first of a group of young people you will soon meet. People you will lead to Christ, and who will help you in your mission. Think of them like your own Disciples. Though they will not leave their lives behind to follow you wherever you go, they will forever be in your debt, and you in theirs. They will touch your heart as deeply and as bravely as you will touch theirs."

She turned back to face the statue of Theresa, placing Thomas' hands upon each side of the smooth, cold stone.

"Your path will cross with Theresa's again in the future. A few times, in fact. It will come at moments when you most need her help." She paused, looking up at him, her eyes filled with nothing but love.

"Now, choose. Which way should she face? Does she represent sorrow? Or joy? You reached out your hands tonight, touched her Spirit, and took away a part of her pain. You gave her the permission to be healed. Do you understand?"

Brother Thomas considered what Saint Thérèse had just told him. He knew she was right. He breathed in deeply, gathering his courage.

"I understand. I may not be able to see my future, but by choosing to see glory in every part of my past, I can affect the direction I am traveling. For tonight, I choose joy. And, if I can, I'd like to go back and choose happiness for my father as well. Not for my own sake, but because I know how much he struggled. He was released from so much spiritual pain, especially the week leading up to his death. If I can, I'd like to change that moment to joy."

He struggled to get the words out, his throat tight as tears began to flow. Thomas choked back deep sobs while he waited for her reply.

Saint Thérèse smiled patiently, nodding softly. "You have always held that power, and that right."

"So, I could change the memory, even now?" he asked, his voice barely a whisper.

"Look," she told him, "it's already done."

Brother Thomas turned to face her, holding her eyes with his. He was hesitant to look behind him. Then, seeing the glimmer in her eyes, he slowly turned to see that what Saint Thérèse said was true. His past had changed. Where before he had witnessed a mixture of struggle and delight, he now saw only glorious blossoms. Both sides of the path, as far as his eyes could see, held nothing but a sea of roses in every color. The beauty and magnitude of the sight caught him completely unaware, and he fell to his knees, crying great tears of joy.

Saint Thérèse allowed him his moment of release, then gently lifted him up. As he stood, he wiped his face on the sleeve of his robe, drying his eyes. He smiled as he let his mind capture this moment.

"Well now. Good thing I'm dreaming. I don't like to cry like that in public," he stated.

She squeezed his hand firmly.

"Come, Thomas. It's time to finish our walk," she said, giving his arm a slight tug.

They walked in silence for a moment, then she spoke once more.

"Tonight was just a dream, Thomas, but come morning, you will remember it vividly. For now, our time is done. I have other souls to visit. Keep in mind always that you hold the power to choose. There will be times that bear great sorrow, but that is life. Let your emotions fill you, and then, let go," Saint Thérèse said, spreading her arms out wide. "Emotions are like rivers. As long as they flow, they stay clean. If we prevent their motion, they become clogged. As long as you feel your emotions, and then let go, you will learn you can always find some joy in every moment, regardless of what it may contain."

Saint Thérèse paused once more, slowing the pace at which she walked. Glancing up, Thomas noticed she had a serious look on her face.

"You've been chosen to undertake a quest, Thomas. A glorious quest that will help fulfill a significant part of God's plan for the world. I do not envy you the road you have been chosen to walk, for you will face events that will cast you into the Dark Night of the Soul, as Saint John of the Cross wrote. But you will also find great glory too.

"Theresa is just one of those who will be with you on this journey. There are many others waiting for you, twelve in all. Young people with their own powers like Theresa."

Brother Thomas gave her a questioning look.

"I'm not sure I follow. Powers? Like a superhero?"

Saint Thérèse looked at him disapprovingly, "I know it's been a long night, but surely you remember what Theresa said. I believe her words were, *'That's when I realized I was invisible, 'cause I ran right between them, and they didn't even look at me.'* Do you not recall?"

"So, her ability to turn invisible…that's real?" Thomas asked incredulously. "I thought it was just a clever metaphor to describe how she felt or something. Are you saying she can really become invisible?"

She chuckled softly, responding, "What fun would there be in a quest if you knew all the answers ahead of time?"

Saint Thérèse paused briefly, considering.

"This much I can tell you: Theresa is being called to great faith, which is why the depth of her pain is equally great. When a pendulum swings, it cannot swing a long distance one way without also swinging an equal distance in the other. She believes there is something out there to believe in, but what she wants to see isn't tangible. To her, it's invisible. And this is why she feels that she, too, must be invisible. For most of my life, I followed a similar path, preferring the company of Jesus to those my age. Theresa isn't hiding because she is afraid of being seen, she becomes invisible so no one will question her faith. And for now, she feels her faith is all she has left. Her pain will bear the fruit of charity in the future, and you will help her see how she can best put that to use.

"Your quest will begin soon. In fact, in some ways, it already has. But it begins in earnest before the full moon rises once more. Where you are going, and what you are to do, I cannot say. I will only tell you this. Trust your faith. Trust that everything you believe, everything you know, even everything that you doubt, it's all real. God is real. Heaven does exist. Not in some far away place in the clouds, or on a distant mountain, or even out among the stars like you considered earlier tonight. It exists here, and now, in this place. And, it exists in all places. These young people you will meet will help you understand this. With them, you will help the world to understand."

She paused, looking Thomas in the eye. "Before you ask, yes, you are up to this. You would not have been selected if God did not have faith in you."

Thomas heard her last sentence the loudest, wondering aloud, "God has faith in me?"

Saint Thérèse stopped walking and tilted her head slightly, smiling broadly at him.

"Strange to think of it that way, yes? But he does. He has faith in you beyond anything you will ever have in yourself. If you only knew the full power of faith. It can move mountains. I know. I've seen it."

She grew quiet for a moment, then continued.

"Remember, Thomas, when you are faced with your greatest challenge, there is only one thing that will overcome: love. Without love, deeds, even the most brilliant, count as nothing."

Brother Thomas recognized her last sentence. He had read it in her book *The Story of a Soul*. It was his favorite quote of hers. He had used it in his opening paragraph of the paper he had written.

Saint Thérèse continued speaking, softer now, her voice fading slowly. "Never hesitate to fall back on love. Even if that seems to be the only thing you have left. Love never fails. Never."

The image of Saint Thérèse was fading. Thomas didn't want her to leave, not now. Not when he still had so many questions. As the last part of her image turned to mist, he heard her voice from everywhere at once.

"Go into the desert, Thomas. Find the Guardians of Zion. God has faith in you."

The dream faded, and Thomas woke. He glanced at the clock on his nightstand. There were only a few minutes left before his alarm would sound. No sense trying to get back to sleep. His mind was filled with questions. Who were the Guardians of Zion? What desert was he headed for? What could be the purpose of his mission?

As if his concerns about his own faith were not enough for him to manage, he now felt as if he held the fate of the world in his hands. Perhaps he did.

*The story continues in Book Two*
*The Paladin of Panama*

Michael Chrobak has been involved in working with Youth and Youth Ministry programs since he was a teen himself; a long, long time ago. He has held the position of Director of Religious Education and Youth Minister for St. Bonaventure's Parish in Concord, CA, and also as Youth Minister for St. Michael's Parish in Livermore, CA. He has survived raising four children of his own and now lives in Oakley, CA where he continues to stay involved in Youth Ministry through his blogs and books.

How to Connect:

Facebook: https://www.facebook.com/michaelchrobakauthor
Twitter: https://twitter.com/MChrobakAuthor
Instagram: https://www.instagram.com/mchrobakauthor
Website: https://michaelchrobakauthor.com

www.ingramcontent.com/pod-product-compliance
Lightning Source LLC
Chambersburg PA
CBHW060434180626
46817CB00007B/2806